EGYPTIAN

The love she had felt for Hugh had died
with him, Noelle knew, and she would
never care for another man again—which
was why she had agreed to please her
parents by marrying Steve Prescott; she
just hadn't any feelings left, least of all for
Steve. Until another woman came along
to make her revise all her ideas about
love . . .

Book you will enjoy
by ELIZABETH ASHTON

REBEL AGAINST LOVE

The first time he met Jo, Marcel de Savigny mistook her for a boy—not surprisingly, because she was the tomboy of the family and scorned all the feminine things like pretty clothes and make-up—and romance. But Marcel persuaded her to go back with him to his home in France to be a companion to his sister—and Jo soon found herself changing her mind about a lot of things!

SILVER ARROW

She should never have married Gray Crawford, Frances thought in despair, however much she loved him. She should have faced the fact that their marriage would be a disaster from the start. For the only love of Gray's life was, and always would be, his speedboat—Silver Arrow.

BORROWED PLUMES

Why should the Greek shipping tycoon Alexander Leandris look twice at plain jane Jan Reynolds when it was her beautiful cousin Renata he was pursuing? Especially as Renata wasn't particularly bothered whether he was offering her marriage or something rather less, and Jan wasn't that kind of girl at all. But then Jan found herself inadvertently aboard Alex's yacht, virtually his prisoner . . .

SICILIAN SUMMER

Niccolo Martelli was certainly a fascinating young man—but he was a rich, aristocratic Italian, while Lucy was only a humble nannie. Surely Niccolo couldn't really seriously care for her? Wasn't it far more likely that he was using her as a smoke-screen to conceal his affair with Lucy's beautiful employer?

EGYPTIAN HONEYMOON

BY

ELIZABETH ASHTON

MILLS & BOON LIMITED
15–16 BROOK'S MEWS
LONDON W1A 1DR

First published 1981
Australian copyright 1981
Philippine copyright 1981
This edition 1981

© Elizabeth Ashton 1981

ISBN 0 263 73578 8

Set in Monophoto Baskerville 11 on 11½ pt.

Made and printed in Great Britain by
Richard Clay (The Chaucer Press) Ltd,
Bungay, Suffolk

CHAPTER ONE

THE bride bent over the register to sign her name, then straightened her back to throw a half frightened glance at her new husband. She was no longer Noelle Esmond, but Noelle Prescott, bound to the enormously successful and wealthy man standing beside her. Every one of the six bridesmaids who escorted her was envious of her good fortune, and threw wistful glances at Steven Prescott's handsome face.

Satisfaction shone in the faces of Jack and Marjorie Esmond, the bride's father and mother, who had both used every argument and persuasion they could devise to bring about this union. Noelle had at last capitulated, and they felt all the relief of a sea captain who had brought his ship bearing valuable cargo safely to port after a hazardous voyage. Even now they could hardly believe that Noelle had at last seen reason and was securely tied to the distinguished man who had courted her assiduously for eighteen months.

Of course it was terribly sad that Hugh Forbes had died in that accident, so young and full of promise, but he could never have provided for their daughter as lavishly as Steve was going to do, and Noelle could not be expected to mourn Hugh for ever. Steve looked magnificent in the full glory of striped trousers and morning coat; he was older than Hugh had been and maturity became him, he was so obviously established and successful. This wedding

in a fashionable London church was a much more
suitable setting for Noelle's beauty than the country
one she had wanted. That was what she had planned
when she was going to marry Hugh, but Steve
wished to show off the loveliness he had won to his
friends, and she had gracefully fallen in with his
arrangements. After all, he was footing the bill for
the reception, which was far beyond the Esmonds'
means. Dear Noelle was so modest, she did not realise
her own worth, but Steve appreciated it. The rope
of pearls about her neck was a token of all the bene-
fits to come.

Noelle herself experienced a moment of panic as
she met Steve's cold grey eyes. She had sworn to
love, honour and obey him, and he was still almost a
stranger to her. The honouring would not be difficult, obedience she was sure he would exact, but
love could not be commanded to order. She doubted
if she could ever come to love him, not as she had
loved Hugh.

Steven Prescott was reputed to always get what
he wanted in the end, by patience and perseverance,
and he had wanted her. He had had to wait for her,
but he had worn down her resistance in the end.
Noelle shivered slightly, wishing she was anywhere
but where she was. She had surrendered eventually
because with Hugh gone, she had not greatly cared
what became of her, and her parents were so set
upon this marriage. Her father's job was insecure
and Steve had promised to find him a better one if
he became his son-in-law, and then there was Simon,
her young brother, of whom she was very fond. Steve
could do so much to give him a good start in life. It

seemed almost selfish to refuse him when he could benefit them all so much, but now, faced with the fait accompli, she was scared by what she had done.

She had been working as a model when she had first met Steve, and Hugh was a designer in Forbes Fashions, the establishment that employed them both. He had been elated when Steve had attended one of their shows escorting a lady who was reputed to be his latest flame.

'He's very generous,' Hugh had said. 'He doesn't mind what he pays for favours given, and as you're much the same build as his lady friend, show off the gowns in your own inimitable style and we'll bag a big order.'

Noelle won more than the order, she excited the escort's interest.

When he asked her out to dinner, Hugh pretended he did not mind. It was good for business for Noelle, wearing one of Forbes' most alluring creations, to be seen in a fashionable restaurant. A dinner would not commit her to anything.

'Insist it must be a public restaurant,' he had warned her. 'No private room or any of that lark.'

Steve was too wily a bird to rush his fences and the girl was shy game. He took her to the Ritz.

Noelle, entrancing in blue crêpe which matched her eyes and enhanced the silvery fairness of her hair, had made her position clear from the start. She was going to marry Hugh and they planned to open their own boutique. Steve listened with an inscrutable expression and encouraged her to discuss her plans. He courteously wished her luck—in matrimony and business, and invited her and Hugh to a party at which he told them some Parisian couturiers would be present whom they might like to meet.

'Are you interested in the rag trade?' Noelle had been surprised.

'I'm interested in many trades and have my fingers in a lot of pies,' he had told her. 'I might perhaps invest in your boutique.'

But there was an avid look in his eyes which Noelle did not like. Hugh was keen to go, and deciding Steve could hardly make a pass at her at a party of which he was host, Noelle went, wondering if the lady of the moment would be present, for Steve was unmarried and his affairs were numerous. Sure enough, a stylish-looking redhead was acting as hostess, who treated Steve with easy familiarity. He took no special notice of Noelle, so it seemed she need have no qualms, and both she and Hugh enjoyed the party which was given in a hotel. Food and drink were lavish, the surroundings glamorous, the company amusing. It was not often they had a chance to indulge in such luxury. After that he was always turning up upon some pretext or the other. Noelle had no reason to suppose he was in pursuit of her, but instinct warned her she was being stalked in a subtle and menacing manner, though what she possessed to interest such a prominent man she could not conceive. Her father had noticed something and bewailed her involvement with Hugh.

'I believe Mr Prescott has taken a fancy to you,' he told her. 'He's offered me a situation in one of his offices, and he asked a lot of questions about you. Just think what an opportunity you're throwing away by wasting yourself on that very ordinary young man!'

'You've no real grounds for such ideas,' she had retorted, 'and I don't aspire to join his collection of fancies past and present.'

'Loose women who don't count,' Jack had commented scornfully. 'He isn't married, and he'll want an heir to his vast commercial empire, and may be looking for a suitable wife.'

'Which I'm not,' Noelle had declared. 'He could marry into society, and I'm only a model girl.'

'Actresses and models have ended up as peeresses before today,' her father remarked pensively. 'Steve will be in the Honours List before he's finished. Lady Prescott.' He smacked his lips. 'You're beautiful, my lovely, modest and chaste, which a lot of them aren't.'

'I'm going to marry Hugh,' Noelle had reminded him firmly. 'So put all these delusions of grandeur out of your head, darling.'

But Hugh had died.

During the service, the words 'till death us do part' had a poignant significance for Noelle. She was not being unfaithful to Hugh, for death had parted them and there are no marriages in heaven. She had mourned for him for a year and a half, and as her parents had pointed out, she must consider her own future. Her pliant, retiring nature was not the stuff of which career women are made. She would never have such a chance again; Steve was rich, handsome and generous. He had offered her marriage which he had never suggested to any other woman as far as was known. Surely she could, in time, come to love him?

But she did not believe he loved her. Love was an emotion difficult to connect with his aloof, rather intimidating personality. He had, after Hugh's death, tactfully avoided her for six months, when he had reappeared and put on the pressure. He often invited the whole family to spend weekends in his fine house outside Maidenhead, which were a great treat for Mrs Esmond, who loved luxury and could leave her household chores. Simon hero-worshipped him, for he rode and shot and initiated the boy into both these sports. He treated Noelle with respect and consideration, but she knew he was biding his time. He desired her, he betrayed that by the expression she occasionally surprised in his eyes, and her reluctance was a challenge. The weekend invitations were only extended if she were included and she had not the heart to deprive her family of so much pleasure, though she feared she might be giving Steve a wrong impression. In time she began to seriously consider accepting him, if he proposed, which was not yet certain. The material advantages of the match were immense, though they did not greatly appeal to her. She would have gladly given all he had to offer for a life of struggle with Hugh, but Hugh was dead, his memory fading, and she desperately needed something to fill the gap he had left. So when Steve did formally propose, she did not reject him outright.

'I don't love you,' she told him frankly. 'My heart is dead since . . . since Hugh died, but I'm lonely.'

'So am I,' he returned unexpectedly.

She had gaped at him.

'Lonely—you? With all your rich friends and . . . and lovely ladies?'

He had smiled sardonically.

'All out to exploit me. But you, I know, are not greedy. You'll make a decorative mistress of this place.' They were in the very beautiful drawing-room of his house, with its long windows looking down to the river, for it was built on a rise in the Cliveden Woods. 'Marry me and I'll make up to you for all you've lost.'

Noelle had shaken her beautiful head.

'Nothing can ever do that.'

Steve had shot her an almost inimical look, knowing she was thinking of Hugh, but he had said suavely:

'Think it over, and consult your family.'

He had made no mention of love. All he appeared to want was a presentable wife to ornament his fine residence.

Her family, she knew, were all for it, especially Simon, who she was determined should benefit, and her mother was not slow to point out all Steve had done and would do for them.

'But I don't love him,' Noelle reiterated.

'Has he asked you for love?' Mrs Esmond had enquired, and Noelle had shaken her head. 'Men of his age have outgrown romantic infatuations, Noelle, and of course he knows you've been bereaved. Don't you want children?'

Noelle did, they would fill her empty heart.

She had been a little at a loss to understand why Steve was so keen to marry her. Then Simon gave her a clue. Steve collected objets d'art. The house contained many cabinets housing his treasures. One morning she and Simon were looking at some bronze figurines, when Simon suddenly opened the door of the cabinet and fished out something from the back of a shelf.

'Look at that, Sis, isn't he a beauty?'

It was a bronze monkey, about eight inches high, perfectly sculpted in every detail. He was standing, with one hand upon a frog, slightly bent, and every hair, every detail of ears, features even the underside of the feet he was standing upon, was perfectly rendered. He was not beautiful, but he was unique.

'Very nice.' Noelle had run her fingers over the smooth metal.

'Steve waited seven years for him,' Simon had told her. 'The owner wouldn't sell. But he got him in the end.' He took the monkey from her and put it back in its place. 'Rum guy, Steve. Once he'd got it, he seems to have forgotten it. It's stuck at the back of the cabinet and I don't think he ever looks at it.'

Noelle had felt suddenly cold. Once Steve had obtained possession of what he desired, did he lose interest in it?

All the same, she accepted Steven Prescott.

He saw no reason for delay, and they were to honeymoon in Egypt. Noelle and Hugh had always wanted to go to that fascinating land, though their chances of doing so seemed remote, but now it was presented to her at the wave of a wand. Steve had told her he would take her anywhere in the world she wished to go, and Simon, who was present, had exclaimed:

'She's always longed to go to Egypt.'

'Then Egypt it shall be,' Steve had promised.

Noelle had wished Simon had held his tongue. The dream of Egypt belonged to her and Hugh, but that was not a reason she could give to Steve for a change of location.

'You're very kind,' she told him later when they were alone. 'And generous. I've so little to give you in return.'

A sudden flame kindled in the usually cold grey eyes.

'I've waited a long time for you, and if you're grateful you can reward me.'

Panic had risen in her, and it was with an effort she resisted the impulse to tear off his ring, the great diamond solitaire he had given her, though it meant going back upon her word.

The flame had died in Steve's eyes, and his gaze was remote and cool as he regarded her.

'You're not a child. You know what marriage is.'

She had nodded her head. To be taken by this man still almost a stranger, to be forced into close intimacy with him . . . could she go through with it?

'I . . . I don't really know you,' she had faltered, trying to excuse her recoil.

'You soon will.' His thin mouth curled cynically. 'Too well, perhaps. There's no experience that doesn't become commonplace with repetition.'

Was he thinking of their wedding night? Was that all it would be to him, an experience that would quickly become stale? Once acquired, would she be put away forgotten in this great house like the bronze monkey, while he sought other diversions? A collection piece, was that all she was to him? She thought she would not much care if she were neglected, she would have her assured position, and possibly a child, and might be glad to be relieved of his attentions. She sighed. It would have been so different if they had been in love, like she and Hugh had been, when consummation would have been shared ecstasy. But that sort of love only came once, and it seemed while she had lost it, Steve had missed out on it. It was unlikely they would ever feel it for each other.

She had known Hugh Forbes all her life, he had been dear and familiar, their mutual affinity fostered by their kindred interest in the world of haute couture. She had inspired his most successful creations and worn them with grace and poise. He had not been very strongly sexed and she was unawakened, so they had agreed not to anticipate their marriage in the modern way, but wait for fulfilment on their wedding night, which would be all the sweeter for the delay. When he had died Noelle had regretted that she had not given him everything before it was too late. Now the unrifled treasure of her body was to be bestowed on this cynical man of the world, for the sake of what he could do for her and hers. In a wave of revulsion against herself and him, she had again made a movement to pull off her engagement ring, but his hard fingers had closed over hers, holding them fast.

'It's too late to change your mind now, Noelle, all the arrangements are made, and I will not permit you to make me a laughing stock.'

'Better a little humiliation now than a lifetime of regret.'

'I'll have no regrets, neither will you once you've put that lost lover of yours out of your mind. He's gone, and I'm sure he wouldn't have wanted you to grieve all your life.'

She was surprised he had so much perception, but

he was deceiving himself if he imagined he could usurp Hugh's place in her affections. Anxious to be completely honest, she had told him so, but Steve had only laughed and told her to face facts, and not be sentimental. That had incensed her.

'Of course a libertine like you are can't appreciate true love,' she had told him recklessly, but instead of being affronted, he had agreed with her. True love as she termed it belonged to the realms of romantic fiction, but Steve was a realist, and she could not expect an adult man, who was a man, to have reached his middle years and still be without experience. She accepted that what he said was logical, only there had been rather a lot of women in his life.

'Then you ought to be flattered that out of them all I've chosen to marry you.'

She supposed she should be, and refrained from remarking that he had only selected her because she seemed suitable at a time when his mind had turned towards founding a family. But he *had* waited nearly two years for her, though he had waited seven for the monkey. Both had been deemed worthy additions to his collection of curios . . . and women. Delay sharpened his desire for acquisition. Steve Prescott did not value the easily obtained.

Noelle had not wanted a fashionable wedding; she and Hugh had planned an early morning ceremony in the church in the village where they had spent their childhood, and she would have liked her marriage to Steve to be as quiet as possible. But her parents went behind her back, having different ideas, her mother telling Steve that a white wedding with all the trimmmings was her daughter's secret wish,

which she had not expressed fearing the expense
might be too much of a drain on her father's pocket,
while her father told Noelle she could not expect an
important man like Steve to agree to a hole-and-
corner affair. So she shrugged her shoulders and let
them make their arrangements with Steve's conni-
vance, feeling it was more their do than hers. The
result of Steve's compliance, and her mother's plot-
ting, was this scene in the vestry, herself in a Paris
gown, bridegroom and best man—a business col-
league of Steve's—in full regalia, and a bevy of
bridesmaids to attend her, mostly connections of
Steve's, for all Noelle could produce was a cousin
from the country. Her friends at the shop were too
bound up with her memories of Hugh to be eligible.
The six girls wore dresses of blue and pink, three of
each colour, high-waisted with puff sleeves, and lace
caps on their heads. They carried small bouquets of
rosebuds, and the bridegroom had given them each
a gold chain.

'Real gold,' said the cousin, Jeannette, awestruck.
She thought Noelle was the luckiest girl alive to be
marrying such a rich and handsome man.

'Like the prince in a fairy story,' she confided to
her aunt.

Marjorie Esmond, an imposing figure in primrose
satin with a turban toque, nodded and smiled.

'Such a happy ending for Noelle,' she said com-
placently, 'after that tragic business with poor
Hugh.'

Privately she considered Hugh's demise had been
a fortunate dispensation of providence. She had
never thought he was good enough for her daughter,

and this wedding was the apex of her ambitions for her, whatever the girl herself might feel. The bride looked lovely in white silk with an Irish lace veil, although she was very pale and there were dark marks under her eyes making them look enormous. Blue eyes and red mouth were the only colour about her, for she had scorned to use a blusher, and with her blonde hair, more silver than gold, she was an ivory bride.

Marjorie Esmond gave a sigh of relief when the ceremony was concluded, for she had feared that at the last moment Noelle might rebel; there had been a faraway look in her eyes all the previous week, and she knew she was living in the past. Now, with the gold band on her finger and the register signed, she was indisputably Mrs Steven Prescott, might even one day be Lady Prescott if Steve was granted the honours that were his due. Mrs Esmond visibly swelled as she considered the pleasure it would give her to refer to her daughter as such.

Her husband was not quite so happy, feeling that a certain amount of coercion had been brought to bear upon Noelle, for they were all indebted to her new husband. She should have looked radiant, instead of which there was a haunted expression in her eyes. She was thinking of Hugh who should have been by her side and not his forceful successor. The good-looking man in his beautifully tailored outfit had no reality for her, though she had just taken his name.

The bridegroom's side of the church was filled with well dressed people, business colleagues and their wives, and among them several fashionable, handsome ladies who had known Steve better than they should have done. Perhaps they had been invited so that he could thus indicate to them their day was done and he was finally committed.

Steve himself had an air of satisfied triumph as if he had pulled off a successful business deal, as in a sense he had. Noelle had not been easy to win, but Steve never accepted defeat. That she had neither birth nor wealth did not trouble him. She had beauty and he could afford to please himself. Steve had come up from the people and won his money and position by sheer dogged perseverance aided by phenomenal luck and an astute brain, for even in these days fortunes can still be made by those who have the know-how. His eyes dwelt upon his bride with possessive pride, a look which caused her to shrink. She did not expect any show of tenderness, that would not have been in character, but he made her feel as if he were a sultan regarding a slave he had purchased in the face of strong competition. He had every right to do so, for that was what she was. In spite of her mother's evasions, she suspected he had paid for most of that day's entertainment.

The couple left the vestry and walked arm in arm down the aisle to the traditional strains of the Wedding March. How primitive it all was, Noelle thought morbidly, the flower-bedecked bride being offered up to a man's lust. Nearly as bad as the last ceremony she had attended—Hugh's funeral. She shuddered as she recalled the finality of seeing the coffin disappear into the grave. She moved on as if in a dream, the floral decorations, the curious eyes were unreal. What was real was her husband's arm beneath her hand and the growing conviction that she had made an appalling mistake. She could never love this man, he was too hard, too cynical and unsympathetic, her heart was buried in the churchyard with Hugh, and she had bound herself to him with the vows she had just spoken. She must have been crazy!

About half way down the aisle, she noticed a striking-looking woman, who was staring at her intently. She recognised her as Marcia Manning, whom Steve had once brought as a customer to the shop where she modelled. She recalled that she had also acted as hostess at his party. Hard green eyes were fixed maliciously on Noelle's white face, while her full mouth curled contemptuously. Her presence was hardly in good taste, for she had been one of Steve's girl-friends, and Noelle could read her thought: A mere model girl when he could have had me. For Marcia was something of a celebrity in her circle and had money of her own.

Then they were past and Noelle forgot her, with the ordeal of the reception ahead of her. This followed a conventional pattern. Refreshments and champagne were served as it was too early for lunch, the newly wedded pair were catching a flight to Cairo before noon. Noelle inserted a knife into the magnificent three-tiered cake, her hand guided by her bridegroom's. There was much laughter and chaffing, as more professional hands took over and cut the required portions. Their healths were drunk, impromptu speeches made. At last Noelle could escape and went to change in the bedroom reserved for her use, with Jeannette's help.

'Oh, you lucky, lucky girl,' her cousin cried. 'How I wish I were you! He's absolutely gorgeous and he'll give you everything you want.'

Noelle stepped out of the shimmering folds of her wedding gown, and reached for the blue linen outfit she had chosen for travelling. Though it was autumn in England it would be hot in Cairo. The dress and matching jacket were simple but beautifully cut. Dispassionately she considered Steve. To Jeannette's unsophisticated eyes he would appear the materialisation of a young girl's dream—handsome, elegant, surrounded by an aura of success and emitting that sexual charm which had enslaved so many women, but beneath all that he was ruthless and callous, for so she judged him, and she wondered if Jeannette had ever noticed how cold those grey eyes could look. But she wouldn't, of course; she was blinded by his glamour, the evidence of his wealth, for which she herself cared not one jot.

'Yes, I suppose I am lucky,' she said without enthusiasm, as she re-fastened Steve's pearls about her neck. She had everything . . . except love, for Steve had never mentioned that. He scorned the tender emotion. He desired her body and wanted to add her to his collection of beautiful objects, that was all.

Jeannette reverently folded the wedding dress which Noelle was leaving behind to be retrieved on her return. The rest of her trousseau was packed in the new leather cases, another present from Steve. Mrs Steven Prescott must travel with luggage suited to her position.

'You're very pale,' she remarked. 'Don't you think you should add a little colour?'

She admired her cousin immensely, she was so lovely and had such a graceful, slender figure. She herself was a little short and stocky, but she seemed oddly unmoved at the enthralling prospect of going away with Steve. Rather she appeared to be remote, wrapped in some dream world of her own.

Noelle glanced indifferently at her face in the mirror.

'It'll do. I've packed my make-up.' She looked at her watch. 'We'd better be going.'

Yet she felt reluctant to leave the sanctuary of the room. Downstairs Steve was waiting and she felt no urge to join him. She had been bought, but the price had still to be paid.

CHAPTER TWO

THEY were served lunch during the flight, the meal arriving neatly packed in the plastic containers used by the airlines.

'Hardly a celebration,' Steve said drily, noticing how little she ate. 'But we'll make up for it at dinner tonight.'

He had insisted that she had the window seat, for Noelle had never been on a longer flight than to Paris. Not that there was much to see, for beneath them were mainly clouds, a billowing mass of grey and white. It had been overcast when they left London. The cabin was filled with the bright light from the sunlit upper sky, a brilliant blue above them. Steve had changed into a lightweight grey suit with a blue shirt, tie and socks. He had taken papers from his briefcase, and after lunch spread them on the table flap before him and became absorbed in perusing them. Though Noelle did not want any amorous demonstration from him, she was a little piqued by his neglect. After all, she was a bride.

'Do you have to do business even on our wedding day?' she asked resentfully.

'I can hardly take advantage of that in a public aircraft,' he returned coolly. 'Haven't you a book or a magazine?'

He had bought a selection at the airport, but they lay unopened on her knees.

Noelle turned her shoulder to him. 'Yes, but I'd rather look out of the window.'

Only the massed clouds met her view.

'I'll have more time to devote to you once I've got these papers out of the way,' Steve told her.

'Oh, go ahead,' she murmured. 'I won't interrupt.'

He turned his head and gave her a long level look under which she wilted. She preferred to be ignored, didn't she, why had she tried to attract his attention? She hastily opened a magazine and became apparently engrossed in it, not realising she was holding it upside down. Steve regarded her drooping head and averted profile with a pleased smile. She was very decorative, this new wife of his, and he had noticed that even among the hurry and scurry of the airport, men had looked at her. He owned what other men desired, which gave him infinite satisfaction. Noelle was unaware of the trend of his thoughts, but she was very much aware of his critical survey. At least her profession had taught her how to dress, her garments fitted perfectly and the colour became her. She looked immaculate and her poise was perfect, he could not fault her there, but inwardly she was quaking. She had told him she did not love him and she had no intention of trying to shirk her marital duties, but would a simulation of passion satisfy him, and could she pretend what she did not feel? He had not married her merely to look at her, nor for the pleasure of her society, which he did not seem to want. She wondered if he realised that she had never slept with Hugh and she was totally inexperienced in sex. However willing she was she feared she might shrink from Steve's touch, which was not the response he would expect from a woman he had bought at some considerable expense. Perhaps if she drank freely at dinner that night it might help.

Steve returned to his papers and Noelle abandoned the magazine for the window. She could see water below them now and here and there an island. The Mediterranean. She and Hugh had planned to visit it some time when they had enough spare cash for a foreign holiday, though they would have had to wait a long time before they could have saved enough to go as far afield as Egypt. Due to Simon's blundering, Steve believed it was where she most wanted to go, and was offering it to her on a plate; that was kind of him, but she had no wish to visit it in *his* company. Ah, if only Hugh was sitting beside her instead of this intimidating stranger! Why, oh, why did he have to be killed? Unconsciously she sighed, and Steve gave her a sharp look.

'Not much longer,' he said, and began to fold up his papers. In confirmation a disembodied voice over the intercom told them they would be landing in fifteen minutes and the sun was shining over Cairo. 'But then it always does.'

Steve returned his papers to his briefcase as they came in over land. As the aircraft lost height, Noelle could distinguish buildings, waterways and roads spread beneath them. Egypt, one of the oldest civilisations in the world, the land of the Pharaohs, where men had lived, loved, fought and died through aeons of history. A country that had been cultured when England was a wooded swamp peopled by barbarians. Noelle felt her pulses stir as the romance of it hit her. Then the lights went on behind the notices forbidding smoking and ordering them to fasten their seat belts. They were arriving.

The hotel where Steve had booked a suite for them overlooked the Nile. It was air-conditioned and seemed almost chill after the heat outside. The suite comprised a sitting room, a bedroom, bathroom and a dressing room. The hotel had recently been rebuilt and was adorned with appropriate murals. Noelle sank into one of the deep armchairs in the sitting room and looked about her. The thick piled carpet was beige, the walls honey-coloured and decorated with pseudo-Egyptian reliefs, of tan-coloured figures in the conventional attitude, shoulders square, faces in profile, dressed in white kilts. There was Osiris, wearing the double crown of Upper and Lower Egypt, holding the crook and flail, sitting in judgment over the departed souls, escorted

by the jackal-headed Anubis. Noelle, who had
always been interested in Egyptology, was pleased
that she had recognised him. Steve wrinkled his
straight nose at the Lord of the Underworld, remarking:

'A bit overdone, isn't it? Like the paintings in a
tomb. Would you care for a drink?'

'Yes, please. Lemonade with plenty of ice.'

He gave the order over the phone.

In a short space of time it arrived in a tall frosted
glass. Service was prompt, the waiter obsequious. He
had learned to recognise quality. Noelle looked curiously at his dark features surmounted by a small
white turban and when he had gone, enquired:

'I suppose they're all Arabs?'

'Yes. The descendants of the original Egyptians
are the Copts, who are mostly Christians, but they're
in the minority.'

Noelle knew that, but did not betray her knowledge. If it pleased him to instruct her let him do so.
She would do anything to atone for the inadequacy
of her feelings towards him. He went on to suggest
that she bathed and changed, she could use the
bathroom first as he had one or two contacts to make.
They would dine early in the hotel restaurant as she
must be hungry after such a poor lunch. Noelle
thanked him for his consideration, though she felt
she never wanted to eat again. Her mouth was dry
as she watched Steve prowling about the room,
commenting upon this and that. He was used to
luxury and critical; she was not, and felt a little
overwhelmed.

Their luggage had been taken into the bedroom

through another door and she went to unpack. The bedroom too overlooked the Nile and was opulently furnished, the dresser having triple mirrors supplemented by a pier-glass; the wardrobes were built in, the whole decorated in white and green. There were twin beds, but each was large enough to accommodate a couple; the quilts were decorated with a lotus flower design. Involuntarily Noelle's eyes kept straying towards them. An early dinner, Steve had said, and then ... the night together. Mechanically she unpacked her cases, shaking out her trousseau dresses. The wardrobe space was all hers, for Steve's luggage was in the dressing room, where apparently he would change. Her own things disposed of, she hesitated. Should she unpack his? It seemed a liberty, but the man *was* her husband and might expect her to do so.

She decided to bath first, and selecting clean nylon underwear went into the gleaming bathroom. The bath was of what looked like white marble, the taps glittered like silver. There was an array of white Turkish towels on the heated rail and an assortment of crystals and bath essences, for the hotel catered for the rich and charged accordingly. The white purity of the room was relieved by a mosaic on the wall beside the bath depicting Cleopatra's arrival at Cydnus to meet Mark Antony. She was shown reclining on cushions in her barge, amidst a wealth of black hair, the traditional gypsy queen, though being a Macedonian she could well have been fair. Recalling that tragic love story, Noelle wondered vaguely if a man could be so infatuated as to lose a kingdom for love of a woman. Certainly Steve never would. If she threatened his business prestige she would very quickly be discarded, she thought wryly. He expected her to enhance it by acting as a gracious hostess and make herself beautiful to impress his friends. That part would not be so difficult, her training would help, but he would also expect reciprocation in bed. Throughout the day he had seemed like a polite stranger, and yet tonight . . . She dragged her thoughts away from the ordeal ahead, and tried to relax. The warm, scented water drew the fatigue of the journey out of her. She had made her bed and she must lie on it . . . with Steve, but she would not think of that until the dreaded moment came.

The dress she put on had wide oriental trousers, with a sequin top that left her arms and shoulders bare. It was in old gold many shades darker than her hair. It was a little daring, but Steve would like that. With it she wore the pearls he had given her, pearl studs in her ears, and the not at all valuable gilt bracelets—Simon's present, the best he could afford, but treasured for his sake. If only her brother were with her now instead of . . . her husband. She coiled her hair on top of her head, encased her narrow feet in gilt sandals, and completed her ensemble with a chiffon scarf, flecked with sequins and gold-fringed. Standing in front of the long glass, she surveyed herself critically. She had put artificial colour on to her cheeks, but had no need of mascara, for by a freak of nature her brows and lashes were dark. She looked a little like an escapee from a harem, she thought, but the exotic touch was suitable to her surroundings.

'Ready to go down?'

Noelle started violently. Steve had come in on noiseless feet and was standing behind her. She must have taken a long time over her toilet, for he was bathed and dressed in a white dinner jacket which showed up his tan, and complemented his black hair. The contrast of his steely eyes in his dark face was always a little disconcerting, and they always seemed to mock. Her first reaction was surprise that he had come unheralded into her room, until she remembered he had every right to come, and without knocking either. She swung round to face him.

'Will I do?'

'Very nice, my dear. The Arabian Nights touch is so suitable for Egypt.'

She saw his thin-lipped mouth curl sardonically. He did not like her dress, she felt sure, and was consequently dashed.

'I thought you'd appreciate something with it,' she said defensively. 'Or would you have preferred virginal white?' And blushed, for after tonight she would not be a virgin.

'Beauty such as yours needs no adornment,' he remarked cryptically. 'I like simplicity.'

'I'll remember that when next I go shopping,' she returned flippantly, reflecting that it would be his money she would be spending. 'Actually this was a model I displayed in our last collection and I was offered it at a reduced price.'

'Price need not concern you in future,' he pointed out, then added belatedly: 'You look very charming, my dear. Shall we go down?'

The dining room was as ornately decorated as the rest of the hotel. The long windows overlooking the river were uncurtained, but tightly closed to retain the air-conditioning. The lighting was subdued, so that as they were seated at a table by the window Noelle could see the water and the lights along its banks, boats like fireflies darting over it, and high in the heavens a few great stars.

The food was excellent, but Noelle had no appetite; in every nerve she was conscious of Steve's presence opposite to her, his eyes wandering possessively over her décolletage. He talked impersonally in his low pleasant voice about the country and the places they must visit, but that was only a disguise for his real thoughts. She drank the sparkling wine he ordered for her avidly, until she seemed to be floating in a dream. Steve refilled her glass without comment, only his smile became more ironic as the meal progressed. When they reached the dessert, her tongue was loosened and she began to chatter, about her family, her work as a model which had terminated with her engagement, her early struggles and disappointments, but she never once mentioned Hugh, who had been the central figure in her past; she had enough discretion left not to do that, though he filled her mind. Steve listened perfunctorily, watching the play of expression across her mobile face, until he said repressively:

'All that is over, my dear, and I hope your new life will compensate you for the deprivations of the old.'

'But I wasn't deprived,' she protested. How could she have been, with Hugh there to support her every inch of the way? Their love and comradeship had lightened the darkest prospect and they had been well on the way up when he had died. But that she could not enlarge upon to Steve, instead she told him:

'It was a fight to get a foothold, but I made good in the end.'

'Ah!' Steve's face lighted up. 'The triumph of achievement—I know the joy of that.' He looked at her oddly. 'And wasn't it your final achievement to marry me?'

Noelle was too confused to understand what he meant or to interpret his probing glance. She had not regarded her capture of Steve as a triumph and his wealth and position meant nothing to her except as a means of helping her family. That she might be considered mercenary did not occur to her.

'We made a sort of bargain,' she said uncertainly. 'We neither of us pretended to be in love.'

'Good God, no!' he exclaimed. 'That folly is for adolescents. I'm long past it.'

'Weren't you ever in love?' she persisted, becoming curious about his love life. There must be some romance.

He shrugged his shoulders. 'Calf love.'

'And all your girl-friends, didn't they love you?'

'Only what I could give them.'

'Did none of them love you for yourself alone?' She would not normally have dared to be so inquisitive, but the wine had emboldened her.

'That,' he said harshly, 'is something I've ceased to expect.'

'Poor Steve,' she murmured, reflecting that she

had been richer than he had ever been, for she and
Hugh had loved without thought of material bene-
fits.

'Keep your pity,' he said scornfully. 'Only failures
need pity. I've acquired all I want without mawkish
sentiment.'

She looked curiously at his hard face with wide
wondering eyes. 'Have you always been self-sufficient? Has there been no softening influence in your
life?'

He shrugged his shoulders. 'I've always had to rely
upon myself alone. My mother was only interested
in my contributions to the household budget. She's
dead now and I didn't mourn her. Softness, my dear,
is weakness.'

A man of granite, Noelle thought with dismay,
and she was his wife. She said faintly:

'You don't need love?'

'Thank God I've grown out of that.'

Well, Noelle thought, she need not reproach herself with having none to give him, but it made their
union all the more distasteful. Passion without love
or tenderness—she shivered.

They had coffee in the lounge and several people
came up to speak to Steve. Noelle realised that he
had stayed there before and had acquaintances in
Cairo. Some of them were women, and very stylish
ones too, who looked at Steve with predatory eyes,
weighing up their chances. He might be with a
woman, but Steve Prescott's fancies never lasted
long. For he introduced his wife informally, merely
saying, 'This is Noelle,' and they thought she was
the lady of the moment. Nettled, she asked him,

when they were for a moment alone, if he were ashamed to own her for his wife.

'Of course not, but I don't want to advertise the fact that we're on honeymoon. There's always something a little embarrassing about that situation or else an occasion for lewd jokes. I prefer to be incognito, as it were.'

She didn't appreciate this explanation, which might or might not be genuine, but she was too weary and fuddled to think it through. Seeing her head nod, Steve suggested it was time to retire, and instantly she became alert. This was the moment she was dreading.

'It's not very late, is it? Couldn't we go out somewhere?'

'My dear, you're dropping on your feet. To-morrow we'll go sightseeing, we're not pressed for time.'

So perforce she must go up to their luxurious suite. He walked with her up the wide staircase, since they were on the next floor it was not worth taking the lift, but Steve did not touch her. Arrived at their bedroom, he said casually, 'See you anon,' and went into his dressing room. Noelle drew a breath of relief; she had feared he would want to strip her himself, as impetuous lovers did in the best romances, but she was to be spared that indignity. She slipped out of her exotic dress which he had not admired into her nightdress and negligee. She brushed her hair and let it hang about her shoulders. She ought to go and clean her teeth, but from the sounds Steve was in the bathroom and she did not want to meet him there. She sat on the dressing stool staring at nothing, unable to bring herself to get into bed. She would try to imagine Steve was Hugh, she thought—wasn't there a saying that all cats were grey in the dark? The idea comforted her.

Steve came in wearing a dark robe, his eyes glittered as they rested upon her slender form drooping over the dressing table, and his nostrils quivered. He did not speak, but reached for her hands, pulling her to her feet. The mirror reflected them, the girl a white wraith against the man's tall dark strength.

'You're somewhat overdressed,' Steve said with laughter in his voice, and stripped off her negligee. It sank, a flimsy mass, at her feet. Her nightgown was long but nearly transparent with only straps over her shoulders. Steve drew a sharp breath, and putting his arms around her drew her close. Noëlle realised then he was naked under his robe, which fell apart, and she was crushed against his bare chest, which was as hard and lean as that of a professional athlete. Noelle closed her eyes and willed herself to be acquiescent, but her body was stiff and inert in his clasp. His mouth wandered over her neck and shoulders, and then to the soft curves of her breasts, which were like those of a waxen image. He sought her lips, which were closed against his kiss. Finally, almost violently, he pushed her away.

'What's the matter with you? Are you a woman or a doll? Didn't that childhood's sweetheart of yours teach you anything?'

Hugh—he was speaking of Hugh, and to mention him in the present circumstances was little short of sacrilege. They had never indulged in heavy petting, somehow there had not been much opportunity, and

Hugh had always treated her with tenderness and reverence. He was, though she had not realised it, a little effeminate, and his urges were nothing like as strong as those of the man she had married. Becoming even paler than before, she said frigidly:

'I'm prepared to do my duty as your wife, but please don't remind me of Hugh.'

She saw a jealous frown gather on Steve's face, and realised too late how her voice had softened when she uttered Hugh's name. She had meant to try to identify the two men as one lover, but knew now such self-deception was impossible.

'Your duty!' Steve almost spat out the words. 'Do you think I want an icicle in my bed?'

'I . . . I can't help it,' Noelle whispered. 'I . . . I told you I didn't love you. I haven't deceived you.'

'But you're a woman, aren't you, made of flesh and blood?'

He seized her again, pressing her against his naked flesh, his hands stroking her body, and deep, very deep within her something stirred, a flicker of flame that died again. If only he had not mentioned Hugh she might have been able to arouse some response, but her dead lover was between them, a ghost of what might have been, whose lips and arms had been so gentle and so loving, entirely different from the fierce demanding passion her husband was betraying. That Steve, normally so aloof and self-restrained, could unleash such a torrent of desire was terrifying. Her lips were bruised from the kisses she had not returned, her body ached from the stricture of his arms. He picked her up and laid her upon the bed, but her body was rigid in his hold, and she turned her face away from him into the pillow, murmuring despairingly: 'I can't.'

She felt his weight pressing down upon her and involuntarily she whispered: 'Oh, Hugh! Hugh!'

She became aware that he had moved off the bed. Turning her head, she stared up at him, where he stood looming over her, a dark, menacing presence. She murmured weakly:

'I'm so . . . sorry. I didn't mean to cheat.'

She wanted to hold out her arms to him, to somehow make amends, for she intuitively knew that she had wounded his masculine vanity; he, the invincible lover, had failed to rouse her. She hadn't wanted to hurt him, even now it was not too late; she could plead virginal recoil—he might not know she was a virgin, from what he had said about Hugh he probably didn't. If he would be gentler, more patient . . . but she could not move; some icy stricture seemed to imprison her, and she could only lie there, staring up at him with eyes like a hunted hare.

Steve laughed harshly, his black brows drawn down over eyes like grey ice.

'Don't mention it, my dear. I don't want a human sacrifice, nor do I want to act as a substitute for the dear departed.' Noelle flinched, for she had had that thought in mind, and he laughed again. 'Keep your memories inviolate, and much good may they do you!'

He wrapped his robe about him and moved towards the dressing room door.

With an immense effort Noelle sat up, forcing a way through the inertia that had bound her. Dismay and regret were mingled with other emotions which she could not define. She only knew that she did not want Steve to leave her like this. Her eyes were big and beseeching, her soft hair falling about her face, while her lips trembled. She looked piteously appealing, but her husband's face remained stony.

'Steve, don't go. I'm so sorry ... I ... can't we ...'

Bitingly sarcastic came his retort:

'Don't put yourself out on my account. I've no use for martyrs.'

'But ... but where are you going?'

'To find a more welcoming bed than yours.'

'At this time of night?'

'Cairo's a nocturnal city. Goodnight, and pleasant dreams ... of Hugh.'

He went through into the dressing room, closing the door quietly but firmly behind him. It had another entrance, so he could leave without her knowledge if he wished.

It was only as he disappeared that the full implication of what he had said hit her. A more welcoming bed ... one of those hussies who had been making eyes at him all the evening, to whom he had introduced her simply as Noelle? Perhaps he had foreseen she might repulse him and had thus left open a way of retreat? Or he might leave the hotel and seek some former love residing in the city. Her frigidity had driven him to it.

But she was not frigid; in spite of her fear and dismay she had experienced a faint stirring of desire in his arms, like the fluttering of a bird seeking to escape. She knew then he did have the power to arouse her, but something had gone terribly wrong.

Was she so poor an actress she could not have faked a response?

It was the mention of Hugh that had petrified her, as if like Banquo's ghost he had risen up between them. The ancient Egyptians believed in the *ka* or double, a sort of astral self that survived death. Had, in this haunted land, Hugh's *ka* come to claim his love? Noelle hurriedly dismissed this fantastic notion. Hugh was the last person to want to wreck her marriage, he would want her to be happy, but her husband was of another breed, proud, jealous, arrogant and unforgiving. He must be supreme, or nothing. That much she had learned about him. Now she had mortally offended him, and this honeymoon had become a farce.

Contrary to her former feelings about Steve, Noelle realised that she very much did want to please him, and the thought of him with another woman was painful to her, but she had not the faintest idea how to effect a reconciliation. Perhaps Steve would not want one, he would find his illicit lovers more satisfactory, and she would merely become a figurehead to entertain his guests, a collector's piece stowed away in a cabinet.

Noelle buried her face in the pillow and wept, feeling humiliated, inadequate and doubly bereft.

CHAPTER THREE

NOELLE awoke to the bright sunlight of another day. No need to wonder if the brilliance of the morning would last throughout the twenty-four hours, as she might have done in England, for here at this time of year no rain would fall, and it was a rarity at other seasons.

The events of the previous night were blurred by sleep, and she was actually in Egypt where she had so longed to be. She jumped out of bed and ran to the window, pulling up the blind to gaze out at the Nile. It would be receding, for the full spate of that life-giving water began in July, though now it was controlled by dams and canals and no longer over-flowed into the city. Inevitably she thought of Hugh. If only he were beside her to enjoy the view, but it was Steven who had brought her and to whom she belonged. Reminded of last night's violence, she glanced at her shoulders in the mirror and saw that they were bruised. Blushing, she picked up her neg-ligee which had been thrown upon the floor by his impatient fingers and wrapped herself in its silken folds. The dreaded night had come and gone and she was alone, having failed lamentably in her duty. She was not entirely to blame, she thought resent-fully. Steve should have made allowances for her innocence; she had never pretended that she loved him, and she had loved Hugh. Had he imagined

that a few expert caresses could wipe out all recollection of her former love? In his arrogant male
pride he had been confident that he could do so,
and now he had gone off in a huff because she had
lain passive in his arms. But not entirely so, and as
she recalled his lovemaking, a shiver of excitement
crept along her nerves. She was instantly ashamed of
it, for she was not a sensual woman, and felt sexuality
was a little degrading.

She looked at his unused bed beside her own.
Should she rumple the covers so that it would look
as though he had slept in it? No need to proclaim to
the staff that they had spent their wedding night
apart, but there was no need for subterfuge. The
chambermaid would think that they had used only
one because she had slept in Steve's arms. Again the
quivering of her nerves, a flutter in her stomach. No,
she was not frigid, and if he had been more patient,
more considerate . . . but no, he had gone off to some
other woman, and her pride lifted its head. She
would not want him back after such an insult.

Noelle went into the bathroom, aware of loneli-
ness. It was very early and Steve would still be with
his inamorata, whoever she was, either in the city or
in the hotel; but only one thing was certain, he was
not in their suite, for when she had bathed and
dressed, she went into his dressing room and saw his
black and gold robe hanging on the door. So he had
gone out, and she knew a moment's panic as it
occurred to her that he might not return. But of
course he would; though their marriage had not been
consummated she was still his wife, and he would
not abandon her however piqued he might be.

A maid brought her a tray of tea. The *effendi* had ordered it the night before, she said. There were two cups and saucers.

'My husband had to go out early,' Noelle told her, 'but he'll be back at any moment,' and hoped she spoke the truth.

The maid withdrew, and Noelle drank her tea seated by the window. She had dressed in tan-coloured slacks and a beige knitted shirt. It was low-necked and short-sleeved. She had no idea how the day was to be spent, but it seemed to be the sort of thing most girls were wearing. She did not intend to spend all morning in the hotel waiting for Steve to turn up, and if he didn't appear she would go out and explore after breakfast. She looked very young and girlish, the sunlight making her hair a gilt frame for her pensive face, her long legs curled under her as she watched the passing craft on the river. Feluccas with their tall distinctive sails mingling with modern yachts and motor launches. She was thinking she would go downstairs, when Steve came in. She heard the click of the sitting room door and his purposeful stride as he came to hers, and she caught her breath, aware her pulses had begun to race when he appeared in the entrance. He was wearing shorts, an open-necked silk shirt, and on his head an Arab headdress, the white draped cloth and braided band. She had yet to learn that they were on sale by every street vendor in the country, and she exclaimed:

'What on earth have you got on your head?'

'A bit of local colour, it's cool and protective. You can buy them for one dollar upwards. This model was two-fifty.' He spoke lightly, and he looked much younger than in his formal suits, seeming sleek and relaxed with no hint of the tensions of the night before. 'Did you sleep well?'

'Very well, thank you,' she replied conventionally, deciding not to enquire where he had spent the night. 'You must have gone out very early.'

'I wanted to watch the sunrise over the Eastern Desert.'

Forgetting their estrangement, she cried, 'Oh, why didn't you wake me? I'd like to have come too.'

'You were sleeping so soundly it seemed a shame to wake you.'

So he must have looked in at her while she slept, and she felt uneasy—suppose she had murmured Hugh's name in her dreams? Whoever Steve had been with, he had not lingered, the sunrise being a greater attraction. That gave her a momentary satisfaction.

'If you're ready, shall we go down to breakfast, or would you prefer to have it sent up here?'

Noelle chose the restaurant, not wanting to be alone with Steve. Though his manner was friendly and he did not seem to bear any rancour, there was a steely glint in his eyes. He had neither forgiven nor forgotten, and she wondered apprehensively what his next move would be.

Over breakfast he told her that he had ordered a taxi to take them out to Giza, for naturally she would want to see the Pyramids and the Sphinx before they left.

'Oh, are we leaving Cairo?' She had left the arranging of their itinerary to him.

'This evening. I've booked accommodation on a steamer up the Nile, it'll be cooler on the water, and you must see Luxor and Karnak and the Aswan Dam.'

'That will be lovely.'

Very deliberately Steve buttered a piece of toast.
'I've booked separate cabins.'

'Oh!' Noelle felt the hot colour flood her face, and
said faintly. 'Did you . . . was that necessary?'

'I think it is.' He raised his head and looked at
her severely. 'Perhaps when this trip is over you'll
have come to regard me less as an ogre and more as
a human being. Until then you'd better sleep alone.'

Noelle's eyes dropped to her plate, aware of con-
flicting emotions. Relief mingled with regret, shame
that he had found her so indadequate, and a curious
sense of flatness that he intended to keep away from
her.

'You . . . you're very considerate,' she murmured.

He returned with suppressed passion: 'I won't
descend to raping my wife, though I've every right
to do so.'

It was still there, the leashed violence that had
scared her. Noelle stirred her coffee with a trembling
hand, looking anywhere but into those avid grey
eyes that seemed to devour her.

'Afterwards . . . it may be different . . .' she said
faintly.

He smiled cruelly. 'Don't try to force yourself to
make it so. You're not indispensable.'

Her eyes widened in dismay. Did he want to be rid
of her already?

'I . . . I suppose you have grounds for a
divorce . . .'

Steve smiled sardonically. 'That comes well from
a day-old bride! I assure you, my love, whatever
happens there'll be no divorce. What I have I hold.'

No divorce, but no love either. She remembered

the bronze monkey which he had long since ceased
to bother to look at. She had been acquired, and
though she might wither in neglect and indifference,
he would never set her free.

Steve's face suddenly cleared, all trace of seri-
ousness vanishing, as he said gaily:

'This is no holiday conversation. Let's be off to see
the Pyramids.'

He sprang to his feet, holding out his hand to her,
looking as youthful and carefree as Simon would
have done. Gone was the urgent lover, the aloof
business executive. His clasp of her fingers was warm
and friendly as they went out of the restaurant.

Before they drove off, Steve insisted upon buying
for her one of the white linen hats on sale everywhere
for those tourists who had underestimated the heat
of the sun. It was not exactly chic, but it did protect
her eyes and nape. Steve continued to appear light-
hearted, even boyish, and Noelle's spirits rose in response. After all, he had given her a respite, and she
might in time come to love him. That seemed possible in his present mood; he had come down to her
level offering her an undemanding comradeship
which she accepted gladly. The trip up the Nile was
going to be fun.

The taxi deposited them at an enclosure opposite
to the Mena House Hotel. Noelle got out, looking
about her in surprise. She could see the bulk of the
Great Pyramid up ahead of her, but where they
stood was a medley of tourists, saddled horses, open
carriages and camels. Steve was giving some instructions to the taxi driver.

'Why are we stopping here?' Noelle demanded.

Steve turned to her with a broad grin. 'Because, my love, we'll approach these historic edifices with due ceremony on camel-back.'

'Ride a camel?'

She wished he would not call her 'my love' with that ironic intonation as if only too well aware it was a misnomer. She wasn't his love; she doubted she ever would be.

'Just so. Much more appropriate than a motor car.'

The camels knelt on the sand, eyeing their would-be passengers with the lofty disdain a camel can so well assume. They were saddled with what looked like red Turkey carpeting and were loud in their complaints when ordered to rise. They were attended by Arabs in djellabahs and turbans assisted by bare-legged boys.

Steve made his requirements known to one of these gentlemen, who salaamed profoundly and assisted Noelle on to one of the humped backs. She was thankful she was wearing trousers, though she hadn't foreseen this exercise. He prodded the beast she be-strode, who staggered to its feet with grumbling pro-tests. Steve was mounted behind her and they were off, plodding up the road, the camels' big splayed feet, designed for travelling on sand, making squel-ching sounds on the tarmac. Their guides ran beside them uttering encouraging noises. The road curved uphill and ended in level sand between the Pyramids. Here her camel knelt and amid grunts and protests allowed her to dismount. Steve was laughing as he settled with the owner.

'They may be the ship of the desert, but they

wouldn't be my favourite form of transport,' he said to her.

'Oh, but it was fun,' Noelle declared, her eyes shining. They turned to look at the great edifices on either side of them, but their majesty was impaired by the invasion of tourists, coaches, shanty shacks and the horde of Arab salesmen peddling souvenirs. Their taxi had followed them, and they drove the short distance down to the Sphinx. Noelle had imagined this great monument would rise in solitary splendour from the desert sand, but it was surrounded by ruined mastabas, the tombs of members of the king's court, some of which were still being excavated. The Pyramids behind it seemed to shut it in and over to the east Cairo was throwing out tentacles which soon would reach to Giza. Added to which, the Sphinx has been badly battered by the passing of the centuries. Steve told her Giza must have been a necropolis and the Sphinx was probably erected as a sort of guardian to protect the spirits of the dead. Sensitive to atmosphere, Noelle drew nearer to Steve, slipping her hand on to his arm, desiring the reassurance of his vitality. He was so splendidly alive in this mausoleum. He looked down at her in surprise; it was the first time she had ever deliberately sought contact with him.

'Something scared you?'

'It's a little creepy, talking about the dead. But I'm very glad to have seen the Pyramids.' She looked up at the great cones piercing the blue sky, and her eyes filled with tears. She had so wanted to see them with Hugh, and he was gone.

Steve with his uncanny perception guessed her

thought, and said curtly:

'You would have preferred more congenial company.'

'Oh no, you mustn't say that,' she protested quickly. 'I'm very grateful . . .'

'I don't want gratitude,' he cut in harshly, pressing her arm against his side, as if to assert his possession of her. 'We'll see if we can get some lunch at Mena House.' He piloted her back towards the waiting taxi, remarking: 'Weird idea to spend so much of one's lifetime preparing one's tomb—rather macabre.'

'They were built by the earlier kings, weren't they?'

'Yes. Chephren or Khufu built the great one, in the fourth dynasty, over two thousand years before Christ. Later on it was realised such tombs were too conspicuous, and they gave them up in favour of rock tombs, which they tried quite unsuccessfully to conceal in the hope of foiling grave robbers. You'll see them in the Valley of the Kings.'

She was surprised at his knowledge. Egyptology was a far cry from his business enterprises, and again guessing her thought, he told her:

'Though I came up the hard way, I found time to acquire some culture.'

'I think you're marvellous,' she said sincerely.

Steve gave her a veiled look. 'So long as I keep my distance, eh?'

'You're not distant now.' She liked the feel of his hard muscles beneath her hand, and she was feeling more in accord with him that at any time during their association. The Arab headdress became him, and he would not make a bad model for a Pharaoh, she thought, with his straight nose and imperious air, though his mouth was too thin-lipped for an Egyptian.

But if I advance too far you'd be off like a scalded cat.'

She hung her head. 'I'm your wife.'

'I won't let you forget it.'

Was that a threat, an invitation, or what? They had reached the taxi and he handed her in without further comment.

As they drove away she remarked, reverting to the former subject:

'After all, all that buried treasure didn't do anyone any good.'

'That's one way of looking at it, and some people must have made a fortune out of their ill-gotten gains, to say nothing of the free meals to rats and mice provided by the offerings of food and drink.'

'Ugh!' She shivered at the picture his words evoked. 'Let's talk of something else.'

'You're too sensitive, my love,' Steve remarked drily. They were sitting side by side, but he did not touch her. Noelle's earlier lightheartedness had evaporated. These monuments were tombs, and her thoughts had winged to Hugh. He had no great pyramid erected to his memory, only a simple slab in a country churchyard. According to the creed of the men who had built the Pyramids he was a lonely shade wandering in Amenti. Had she betrayed him by marrying Steve? Steve glanced at her still, remote face, and observed:

'You're being morbid. The dead have no claims on the living.'

She did not like the way he seemed able to read

her thoughts; his were a complete enigma to her. She turned towards him with an apologetic smile.

'I'm sorry to be such a wet, but I'm rather tired. It was lovely seeing all this, but a bit exhausting.'

'Sightseeing always is,' he said prosaically. 'Especially in this heat. This afternoon you must lie down and rest.'

She revived over lunch, and the Mena House Hotel was quite something with its Moorish arches and well tended gardens. Steve talked about the places they would be visiting and the great temples at what had been the capital of the Middle Kingdom, Thebes, that was now called Luxor. He seemed to be deliberately trying to be impersonal. Finally he told her:

'Antiquity has always interested me, and I collect objets d'art. You've seen some of my collections at Cliveden?'

She remembered the bronze monkey.

'Yes. You're very patient when you're set upon acquiring something.'

He shot her a meaning glance. 'I am. A valuable object is worth waiting for.'

'Do you include me in that category?' she asked provocatively.

He laughed genially. 'That's fishing. People aren't things.'

Noelle obediently tried to rest during the afternoon. Steve conducted her to the bedroom and said he would call her when it was time to go to the boat. He would ask the chambermaid to pack for them. Then he left her, and she wondered where he was going. She felt restless and over-stimulated, but finally she dozed and dreamed. She was in a tunnel leading into the interior of a tomb and Steve was beside her. It was dark and cold and she was scared. 'Please,' she besought him, 'let's go back into the sunshine.'

He laughed low and mockingly as he replied:

'There's no going back, my love.'

She awoke to find the chambermaid packing her cases as requested, and changed into a white dress with a white woollen wrap, since it might be cool on the water. The maid was a plump dark woman, not at all young, and was deft and efficient. She insisted upon running a bath for Noelle. Unused to being maided, Noelle was a little embarrassed, especially when the woman—she said her name was Miriam— exclaimed over her white skin and pale gold hair. She was packing Steve's suits, far more expertly than Noelle could have done, when Steve came in. He had discarded his shorts and headdress and was wearing white trousers and a blazer. It seemed he and Miriam were old acquaintances, and she looked at him with dark melting eyes, thinking of the large tip he would give her.

He regarded Noelle's ensemble with approval, obviously preferring it to what she had worn on the previous evening. He looked so handsome and dis-tinguished that Noelle felt her pulses stir. If he came to her tonight she would try to give him a warmer reception. Then she remembered the separate cabins, and felt quite inexplicably dashed. She ought to be thankful for his forbearance, but contrarily she began to wonder if she had alienated him to the extent that he no longer desired her. She searched his unrevealing face for some clue to his feelings, but his grey eyes were as clear as glass and as expressionless.

If they had been alone, she might have made an advance, but Miriam's presence prohibited any intimacy. He chatted with the Arab woman in a friendly manner, asking about her husband and children, for Miriam was a married woman. Noelle was pleased to learn that Steve had no side where dependents were concerned, though she had heard he could be a terror in his office. But that was different, she supposed, in business he had to impose his authority.

The sun had sunk when they reached the quay where the Nile steamer, *Serapis*, was berthed. She was an odd-looking craft, more like a floating hotel, with three decks connected by outside staircases, and a promenade around each of the three tiers of cabins and saloons. Behind them the sky flamed over the Western Desert and was reflected in the water so that the boat seemed to be floating on a sea of fire.

Steve and Noelle descended from their taxi, while a horde of porters seized their luggage to carry it to their cabins. Other passengers were arriving, being decanted from their cars, and followed them to the ship. As she went up the gangway, Noelle looked back and encountered a pair of malicious green eyes under curled red hair.

'Hi, Steve!' the woman called in a throaty sexy voice. 'Are you going on this trip? What a bit of luck!'

'Marcia!' Steve's surprise was well acted, but with a stab, Noelle didn't believe it was genuine. 'We can't talk here. See you later.'

He piloted Noelle on to the deck, where a steward was waiting to conduct them to their cabins.

Noelle's mind was seething with questions. So Marcia Manning was also in Egypt. Had she followed them, knowing their destination? There had been a false note about their greeting, and Noelle was convinced her husband had expected her. She glanced at his face, which was a little grim, and the awful certainty gripped her that it was to Marcia he had gone last night when he had left her. He knew she would be in Cairo. No wonder he had looked so sleek and contented when she met him at breakfast!

They had adjoining cabins in the stern of the top deck, opening on to a small promenade deck furnished with deck chairs. The accommodation was comfortable, though small, with their own tiny bathroom containing a shower. There was a connecting door between their cabins, and it was open as she was ushered in and Steve came through it, as she stood by the window trying to collect her thoughts.

'This seems all right,' he said, looking round critically. 'There's a bar further aft. I'll meet you there, when you've unpacked what you'll need tonight. There's not a lot of cupboard space.'

Spoken oh, so casually, as if no red-haired siren had come aboard at his invitation. Noelle swung round to face him, her eyes blazing sapphires in her pale face. Marcia's presence was an insult she could not forgive.

'You knew she was coming, didn't you?' she accused him. 'Perhaps you booked her ticket when you booked ours. Do you usually travel with a harem so that if one houri disappoints you you've a replacement to fall back upon?'

Steve took a stride towards her and gripped her shoulders with fingers of steel.

'What the hell are you talking about?'

'Marcia Manning, of course.'

'Oh, her!' Was it her fancy or had a wary look come into his eyes?

'Yes, her!' Anger and humiliation made Noelle reckless. 'Do you think I don't know she's your ex-mistress, only I doubt the ex. Was it her bed that welcomed you last night?'

A flash of anger crossed his face, and he shook her violently.

'What a thing to say to your husband!'

'Who isn't a real husband; I wouldn't mind so much if it were anyone but her.'

'You wouldn't?' He dropped his hands and his face became like the carved stone of an Egyptian statue. 'So you've some passion in you, but I hardly think you're in a position to criticise my actions.'

Noelle flushed and hung her head; she had antagonised him with her mention of Hugh, and she did not really blame him for seeking satisfaction elsewhere, but not with Marcia Manning who, she knew, despised her, the girl who had modelled for her when she came to buy clothes at Forbes Fashions, clothes which she was fairly certain Steve had paid for. Marcia who had acted as hostess at his party. She could not bear to think that Steve might confide her inadequacies to his former mistress—or was she still his present one?

Steve went on quietly:

'I've no control over Marcia's comings and goings, and it's bad luck she should turn up here. I'm afraid you'll have to put up with her presence, which is none of my contriving, I assure you.'

Noelle lifted her head defiantly. 'I don't believe you.'

'You don't?' He made a movement towards her, and she stiffened, expecting some violence, but he controlled himself. He shrugged his shoulders and told her: 'Believe what you please, it won't alter facts.'

'No, neither will you pull wool over my eyes. I learned the facts of life in the modelling world. I had a good education in the habits of wolves, and you were a prime one before you decided to get married. You can't deny it.'

He thrust his hands into his trouser pockets and eyed her coldly.

'I deny nothing, but don't dare to blackguard me. I won't stand for it.'

'Why, what would you do?'

'Do you want to challenge me?' He caught her roughly in his arms, staring down into her face while he deliberately crushed her against him. Noelle felt a trembling in her limbs, her body going limp, and then she recalled that those same arms had held Marcia last night. She became stiff as a ramrod.

'Force will get you nowhere,' she whispered. 'Do you want to make me hate you?'

He pushed her away from him with a muttered oath.

'I might say the same to you.'

The decks shuddered under their feet as the ship

began to move away from the quay and Noelle realised her retreat had been cut off. She had been about to declare that she would not stay aboard with Marcia Manning, but now it was too late. Her pulses still throbbed from Steve's fierce embrace, and she pushed the heavy hair off her forehead with a weary gesture. After all, what did it matter? Steve was bound to take up with some female since she had failed him, but she had begun to hope that she might be able to respond to him if he approached her again. Now they were quarrelling, saying things neither would forgive.

'I'm sorry I lost my temper,' she said quietly. 'But I had provocation.'

'So you've made yourself believe.' Steve had become cool and suave, entirely unrepentant ... Noelle had a wild impulse to hit him with her hairbrush or scratch his smooth, mocking face—anything to break that imperturbable calm. But her hairbrush was still unpacked and she had never scratched anyone in her life. 'You'll feel better when you've had some dinner,' he went on. 'When you've tidied yourself, we'll go and sample the restaurant.'

For her hair was hanging about her face, and her make-up smudged.

'I don't want any dinner,' she muttered.

'Oh, don't be childish,' he said impatiently. 'Do you want Marcia to think we've quarrelled?'

'I don't care what Marcia thinks,' she snapped, but she did. If Marcia thought they had disagreed, she would be triumphant, and if Steve went into the restaurant alone she would join him. She had not appeared to have anyone travelling with her.

Mechanically Noelle moved to the dressing shelf, it was not much more than that, and began to re-arrange her hair. Then she touched up her make-up, while Steve watched her, standing coolly aloof with folded arms.

Then he said firmly:

'Whatever your private feelings I expect you to behave with dignity in public—you owe it to my position as well as your own. You must be polite to Marcia, however inopportune her presence is—we don't want to advertise our personal relationships to the whole ship's company. Now, if you're ready, we'll go to dinner, and please try to act like a demure little bride and not like a termagant.'

Noelle's heart swelled with indignation. He did not care how outraged she felt so long as she pre-served a façade of wedded bliss. Resisting a desire to smack his face, she turned from the inadequate mirror and said sweetly:

'I'm ready to accompany you.'

But you wait, she thought angrily, somehow I'll get even with you!

They descended the stairs to the lowest deck where the restaurant was situated, and before they entered it, Steve crooked his arm, and she laid her hand within it. A waiter indicated their table and pulled out her chair for her. Noelle seated herself sedately opposite to her husband, a picture of wifely submis-sion, but when she raised her eyes to his face, they were sparkling with suppressed fury.

CHAPTER FOUR

NOELLE'S indignation gradually subsided in the face
of Steve's bland indifference. Like all emotions it
needed stimulus to stoke it, and short of repeating
her accusations, which seemed to have made no
impression on him, the only course left to her was to
retreat into dignified silence. One cannot have a row
if one's opponent won't play, and a public dining
room was not the place for altercations, as she had
already been told. She was not of a sulky disposition
and she found herself responding politely to Steve's
chit-chat as if nothing provoking had occurred.
There was a humorous gleam in his eyes as if he
were well aware of her suppressed feelings. That they
amused him added to her rancour, but she betrayed
no outward sign of it.

It helped that Marcia was not visible. The small
dining saloon was full, and if she was there she was
concealed by the other diners. Noelle had half expected that she would approach them and request a
seat at their table, although it was only laid for two,
but she had not done so, and Noelle began to wonder
if her presence on board was in truth a coincidence,
thereby lessening Steve's offence, but she was still
convinced he had known Marcia was in the Cairo
hotel, and he had had her in mind when he had
taunted her about a more welcoming bed.

Nobody was wearing evening dress, though most
of the women had put on skirts or dresses. Since it

was an expensive trip, the majority of the passengers were middle-aged, but a younger man at a nearby table attracted Noelle's attention, principally because he kept staring at her.

Although he was clad in European dress, a light-weight grey suit with a collar and tie, he was obviously of Eastern origin. His very black hair, liquid black eyes and brown skin could have been Spanish or Italian, but somehow he did not look like a Latin. Noticing the direction of her gaze, Steve looked round and saw him.

The man smiled, disclosing very white teeth, and raised a long-fingered brown hand in salutation displaying a gleam of gold cuff links in his immaculate white shirt, and Steve nodded to him.

'You know him?' Noelle asked.

'Oh yes, he dabbles in all sorts of things. He's Omar ben Ahmed, a princeling from one of the Oil States. What you might call a playboy of the Eastern world. I shouldn't have thought this trip would have been exciting enough for him.'

'He's handsome,' said Noelle, giving the man a provocative glance. 'And I suppose he's rolling?'

'More money than sense,' Steve growled, scanning his wife's pale beauty with a frown. He knew how it would appeal to the dark Lothario across the way.

'Married?' Noelle enquired nonchalantly.

'Probably. He's allowed four wives, and divorce is easy—for the man—in Islam.'

Noelle played absently with a spoon, a half formed project in her mind, she didn't think Mr Ben Ahmed would need much encouragement to be . . . friendly.

'Women are still second-class citizens in his

country,' Steve went on, 'and infidelity on the lady's part is severely punished.'

'So unfair!'

Steve shrugged. 'What would you? A man likes to be sure his children are his own.'

'Nowadays there needn't be children, but all the same it's still a man's world. Men everywhere have the best of it, except possibly in America.'

Steve laughed indulgently. 'A profound statement, my love!' Again the derisive intonation. 'But you've hardly had enough experience at your age to be an authority on the subject.'

Noelle met the eloquent eyes of the dark man.

'I could gain it,' she said meditatively.

Steve returned silkily, 'Though I promised I won't force myself upon you, you're still my wife, and I won't condone extra-marital strayings.'

On her part, but what about himself? Noelle threw him a mutinous glance, and turned her head towards the moonlit scene outside through the window beside her. The silvered water glided past with a dimly visible coastline on the farther bank. Palm trees were etched blackly against the lighter sky, with here and there a village, its position marked by a few points of light.

A man's world.

They were finishing their coffee—Turkish, served with the grains left in and very sweet. One only drank half the cup, and Noelle decided she did not like it much, when Omar ben Ahmed rose from his seat and came to their table. He was not very tall, but his shoulders were broad, his expensive suit beautifully cut to show off his slim elegance.

Steve stood up, and both men bowed, exchanging greetings in what Noelle supposed was Arabic. Then the bold black eyes went to Noelle's face, as he said in perfect English:

'Present me to Madam.'

Steve's face was expressionless as he introduced them, but his grey eyes were watchful.

'Perhaps you would both take drink with me in the upper bar,' the Arab went on. 'As you see, I'm on my own.'

'Thank you, I'd be pleased to join you,' Steve said suavely, 'but my wife is tired. She's going to bed.'

'I'm not all that tired,' Noelle contradicted him, 'and I'd like a drink.' She smiled at Omar.

'Madam is gracious to take pity on a lonely bachelor,' he told her, bowing again.

Steve gave her a quelling look but made no protest. The three of them left the dining saloon and ascended to the upper deck, Omar gallantly assisting Noelle with a hand under her elbow. She did not object, for she knew his action annoyed Steve and she was taking her revenge for Marcia.

Arrived in the bar, Steve rather ostentatiously sat down between them as the waiter came for their order.

The Islamic ban on alcohol did not seem to worry Omar, for he asked for a bottle of champagne.

Then Marcia came into the bar. She was wearing a scanty green dress with a slit skirt and a deep décolletage. Her red curls were loose upon her shoulders and she was heavily made up, the lines round her eyes drawn out to the edge of her cheeks, giving her a slightly sinister look. Green eye-shadow above them intensified their hue.

She saw them at once and came towards them, swaying her hips.

'Three's no company,' she drawled. 'May I join you to make the number even? I'm on my own.'

Both men rose to their feet.

'We can't allow such a beautiful lady to be neglected,' Omar told her. 'We shall be honoured if you will drink with us.'

Marcia sat down on the chair Steve had vacated next to Noelle, who caught a whiff of her expensive scent. Marcia was in full warpaint and out to kill, though whether her quarry was Omar or Steve was not apparent. They rearranged themselves, and now Noelle had Marcia on one side of her and Omar on the other, with Steve opposite to her. Omar's thigh was pressed against hers, either because space was restricted or intentionally. She made no movement to draw away, for Steve was gazing into Marcia's green eyes with an amorous expression. Two can play at that game, she was thinking, and I'm not going to act the neglected wife. What's sauce for the goose, etc. But it was not on the Arab her thoughts were fixed, but upon her errant husband. What was Marcia's lure for him? The woman was an obvious gold-digger, and though her appearance was striking, it was not in the least refined, hardly what would be expected to attract Steve, who was famed for his good taste. She must be good in bed, and Noelle sighed. That was a region in which she was still a novice, and seemed unlikely to be initiated.

The champagne foamed and bubbled in their glasses and tongues were loosened. Omar plied Noelle with flowery compliments. Marcia leaned forward so that Steve could have a good view of the cleft between her breasts and laid her hand beside his on the table.

'The friends who were to have joined me on this boat decided at the last minute to fly to Luxor,' she told them with a woebegone expression. 'So I'll be all on my own until we get there. I'm sure your wife won't mind if you look after me, Steve, since we're such old friends. I'm such a fool about tipping and ordering meals, and the stewards always try to ignore a woman alone.'

Which was blatantly untrue, and Marcia was fully capable of looking after herself. Noelle glanced at Steve—surely he was not going to fall for this helpless little woman act?—and saw he was smiling complaisantly, so apparently he had. Irritated beyond endurance, she drained her glass and with a bright spot of colour on either cheek and her blue eyes sparkling, she said sweetly:

'If you mean you want to borrow my husband until we reach Luxor, you're welcome to him. I can amuse myself quite well without him.'

Marcia gave a start of surprise, then said:

'You're very generous. I may take you up on that.'

The renewed pressure of Omar's knee showed that he had grasped the situation. Noelle knew she had spoken out of turn, but if Steve meant to continue his liaison with that brazen bitch, she would prefer that he did so openly without trying to deceive her.

Steve stood up, with a brow like Jove about to deliver a thunderbolt.

'Go to bed, Noelle,' he commanded. 'You're high.'

She looked up at him defiantly, but she did not

move. She had drunk rather a lot of champagne, Omar had kept surreptitiously refilling her glass. It had made her reckless.

'Perhaps you'd better go and lie down,' Marcia purred. 'You perhaps didn't realise champagne is so potent.'

'Thank you, you don't have to tell me that,' Noelle returned with immense dignity. 'I'll go to bed when I feel like it.'

'You will go now!'

At the rasp in Steve's voice, both women looked at him apprehensively. Then Omar said quickly:

'Let me escort you to your cabin, madam.'

'Thank you, but I'll do that,' Steve told him. His eyes were dark with anger, his mouth set like a steel trap. A little uncertainly, Noelle rose to her feet.

'A sh-shame to break up the party, but I've sworn to obey him.' She giggled. Steve's hand closed over her arm like a vice. 'S-see you in the morning, folks.'

He propelled her out of the room from whence it was only a short distance to her cabin. The cool night air as they went along the deck sobered her, and she glanced anxiously at her husband, wondering what he was going to say to her. They reached her cabin, and pushing her inside, he followed her, closing the door after him. Noelle walked across to the window, closed against marauding insects, and leaned her forehead against the cool pane, as Steve spoke.

'I'd be quite justified if I took off my belt to you. How dare you make such an outrageous suggestion, and behave so disgracefully!'

'Beat me if it'll relieve your feelings,' she returned

without looking round. 'It seems I've married a tyrant with no regard for mine. You'd better hurry up and administer my punishment, or Marcia will go off with that desert sheik. I don't suppose she's particular so long as she's got a man.'

'Your suppositions are quite absurd,' Steve reprimanded her, 'and it isn't Marcia who's caught Omar's eye.' He put a hand on her shoulder and spun her round to face him. 'I can only surmise you're mad jealous of her.'

Noelle went off into peals of hysterical laughter, and Steve slapped her face. Pulling herself together, with one hand to her smarting cheek, she said disdainfully:

'Jealous of that tart? You flatter yourself. I don't care who you sleep with so long as it isn't me.'

Steve went quite white, and his eyes blazed, then with a muttered oath he went out, slamming the door behind him.

Noelle sat down on her narrow bed and found she was shaking. She had done it now, good and proper, but she felt no elation. She had behaved badly, but Steve had spoken to her as if she were a naughty child, to be sent to bed for her misdemeanours, and Marcia's effrontery had infuriated her. Was she expected to spend her honeymoon à trois? It was too much to expect of a new wife, even if she were only a wife in name. Steve had been so different that morning during the expedition to Giza, almost she had been on the verge of capitulation. She had been looking forward to seeing Luxor and Karnak in his company, believing that they might arrive at a better understanding amid the mutual interest in the ruins.

But Marcia had turned up and spoilt every hope of a closer union. Steve had declared her suppositions were absurd, but his every action confirmed them. Even Marcia would not have dared to thrust her company upon them if she had not had previous encouragement. *Of course* Steve had known she would be on the boat, and her story about friends meeting her at Luxor was a fabrication. Well, they could have their fun and Noelle wouldn't try to intervene. As she had told him she did not care as long as he left her alone.

Alone—what a dismal word! Ever since Hugh had died she had felt so much alone. Though she had not expected much from her marriage to Steve, she had hoped for children, but there was no prospect of a family if he continued to seek his satisfaction elsewhere. She looked round her single cabin with lacklustre eyes. Its prim neatness emphasised her solitude. But she didn't want Steve to relieve it, certainly not, but there was Omar ben Ahmed. He was disposed to be friendly, though Steve had plainly disapproved, but fair was fair. Since she was quite indifferent to the princeling, she could be in no danger from him, and Steve had no right to object when he had Marcia. It would salve her pride to have an attendant cavalier to flaunt in front of Marcia's supercilious eyes.

She stood up to prepare for bed. The cabin, being a single one, had its own shower and so on in a cubicle in one corner. The door between her and Steve was firmly locked. She opened the one leading out on the deck and went outside. Steve's adjacent one was dark; he was probably still with Marcia, and afterwards would go to her cabin. Noelle leaned over the rail looking at the water swirling past. The moon was full, a golden orb in a velvet sky ... a honeymoon. The faint throb of the engines was audible as the unwieldy craft pursued its way upstream, and the deck vibrated a little under her feet. It was not private, it had access to the lower decks, but she had it to herself tonight. She was a tiny atom in this great mysterious land, being borne up this most romantic of rivers to ... what? Further humiliations at Luxor? Gradually the calmness of the night soothed her battered feelings. She glanced towards Steve's cabin—still no light—then with a sigh went back into hers.

Tired with all the excitements of the day, she was soon asleep, but as towards dawn she half awakened, before turning and sinking into sleep again, she uttered a man's name, but it was not Hugh, it was Steve.

Breakfast could be served in one's cabin if one so desired and did not want anything cooked. Noelle availed herself of this service next morning, the steward bringing her a tray of coffee, rolls and fruit. By doing so she avoided meeting anyone. When she was dressed, she went out on deck, where canvas chairs had been set out.

The *Serapis* was not a luxury boat like the Nile-Hilton streamers that plied between Luxor and Aswan. The more usual method of touring by those anxious to see as much as possible in the time available was to fly to the former town and take the boat there. Cairo had been still very hot and Steve had thought the all-river trip would be cooler and more

relaxing, and since the *Serapis* had accommodation
to spare he had booked it. That was what he had
told Noelle, but after Marcia's appearance she was
sure he had made an assignation with her and her
story about friends letting her down was but a flimsy
excuse.

This morning Noelle was not to have the deck to
herself; an elderly couple had already availed themselves of its seclusion. English, she thought as she
met their slightly hostile stare. The English always
resented intrusion, while Continentals welcomed it.
She bade them a polite good morning and the man,
perceiving she was a pretty girl, responded with a
smile.

'Good morning, my dear. I'm Colonel Bates and
this is my wife.'

'And I'm Noelle Esm . . . Prescott.' She was not
used to her new name. She sat down on a lounger
beside the Colonel, unwilling to go farther afield in
case she encountered Steve and Marcia. They exchanged the usual small talk. Then the Colonel tilted
his straw hat over his eyes and began to doze. Mrs
Bates chatted on about their country cottage in
Devonshire; her children, now married, had settled
elsewhere. Her hands were busy with cotton and
hook; she was crocheting lace. Noelle listened idly,
watching the landscape slipping by. This part of the
Nile wound through rocky cliffs, which surprised her,
as she had expected to see flat sands. Villages clus-
tered at the water's edge, amid palm trees and tam-
arisks; these with casuarinas and eucalyptus were the
only arboreal products of Egypt, where there were no
forests of hardwood trees. The natives used camel

dung for fuel. It is a mainly agricultural country; cotton, cereals and rice flourish, but principally in the Delta region. In classical times Egypt was one of Rome's chief granaries. The villagers' houses are built of mud brick with unglazed square or round windows. Usually several are joined together, and the flat roofs are used to store everything from mattresses to bundles of reeds, which give them a derelict look. Life among the *fellahin* must be very primitive, Noelle reflected, and felt a little ashamed of the luxury with which she was surrounded. But they did have continual sunshine and warmth to make their lives easier.

She was half asleep when she suddenly became aware that the engines had stopped and the boat was drifting gently back downstream. Mrs Bates was looking alarmed.

'Harry, wake up,' she called. 'We've stopped. Something must be wrong.'

Her husband opened one eye. 'Damned inefficient wogs,' he grumbled. 'Don't panic, my dear, I expect it's only engine trouble.'

'You don't think the boat might blow up?'

'Most unlikely. We've probably run into a crocodile.' He laughed facetiously.

Noelle sat up and listened. She heard raised voices and splashing up for'ard.

'Do go and see, Harry,' Mrs Bates insisted. 'I'm sure something's happened.'

The Colonel raised himself reluctantly on one elbow, but at that moment the engines started up again and the boat began to move in the right direction.

'There, you see, nothing to make a fuss about,' he said as he settled down again.

The sun increased in power, and Noelle decided to seek the comparative cool inside the lounge. Her companions, who had said they were used to the tropics, seemed impervious to heat, but she had never been able to stand too much sun. Bidding them au revoir, she went down to the lower deck. Green blinds shut out the glare from the lounge and made the light dim. Noelle paused inside the entry, blinking, and a voice beside her made her start violently.

'Good morning, beautiful madam. I trust you slept well. You look fair as the sunshine.'

'I don't feel it,' Noelle returned, 'it's getting very hot.'

As her vision adapted itself to the change of light, she saw Omar ben Ahmed standing in front of her. He was wearing a white suit and his dark eyes glistened as they raked her from head to foot, taking in every detail of her supple figure clad in a plain blue dress, her white sandals and her hair loose upon her shoulders. Reaching out, he touched a tress of it.

'Pardon me, but it fascinates me.'

Noelle jerked her head away.

'I should have put it up, but it's so hot. Where is everybody?' For the lounge appeared to be empty.

'Either sleeping off last night's excesses or sun-bathing,' Omar told her. 'After you went last night, more champagne. We broke up very late. The green-eyed one has an infinite capacity.'

Noelle turned her head away. Steve, of course, had rejoined Marcia after he had left her.

'But what would you,' Omar went on. 'There is

nothing else to do. But sit down, fair one, and allow me to order you a drink. Coffee?'

'Yes, please, but not Turkish.'

She sat down on a banquette with a low table in front of her. Omar procured two cups of coffee, then seating himself beside her said:

'Now tell me all about yourself. You are newly married, yes?' He glanced at her ring. 'Your husband is an old acquaintance of mine, we have dealt together.'

Noelle recalled that the men had greeted each other in Arabic, and remarked: 'He speaks your language.'

'Yes. I believe Steven Prescott knows something about everything, except how to treat a wife.'

The black eyes were insinuating, but Noelle did not rise. She was not going to confide in this Arab Don Juan. She said carelessly:

'I expect you aren't used to our Occidental manners.'

Omar laughed. 'They are strange to me, but Steve is of the West and I am of the East, and as your poet says, never the twain shall meet, except perhaps in love. You love him very much?'

Noelle looked down into her cup. The question verged on impertinence, and if she answered it truthfully she would have to say that love had no part in her marriage, but neither did it in Eastern unions, which were almost always arranged. The admiration in his eyes was balm to her wounded pride.

'He's a very successful and clever man,' she said evasively. 'Have you seen him this morning?'

'Oh yes, but weren't you present when he per-formed his heroic rescue act?' His tone was mocking.

Noelle stared at him. 'Rescue act? What are you talking about?'

'So you weren't? How disappointed he will be!'

Sudden anxiety gripped her. 'Oh, please be seri-ous! I know the boat stopped—tell me what hap-pened. He's all right?'

'There was a little altercation on the stairway be-tween an irate passenger and a waiter, who he said had tried to cheat him. Blows were struck and the fellow fell overboard. He could not swim, so Steve dived in after him. Quite unnecessary, there are plenty of lifebelts.'

Noelle stood up; she had gone very white. This was what had been happening while she had chatted unconcernedly with the Bates. Steve had been in danger and she completely unaware.

Omar said soothingly: 'Don't distress yourself, madam. They fished them both out and the whole episode was over in moments.'

'But . . . but . . . the crocodiles!' she stammered, her eyes widening in horror as she recalled the Colonel's words.

Omar laughed again. 'They were all made into shoes and handbags long ago.'

'Oh! But where is he? I must go to him.'

She might not love him, but he *was* her husband, somebody should have informed her. Omar was making light of the incident, implying that Steve had been showing off, but he might be injured, shocked, needing her.

Omar touched her arm gently to check her.

'The green-eyed houri is fussing over him. In my opinion he only did it to impress her.'

Noelle sat down again abruptly. So Marcia had witnessed the whole performance, though she did not believe she had been the motive for Steve's rash action. Possibly there had been no real risk; Steve was a strong swimmer. Marcia had usurped her place, without sending to tell her. Quite likely Steve had not wanted her.

Omar looked at her sympathetically and laid his hand over hers. She looked at it dully, but made no movement of withdrawal. She was surprised how upset she had been to learn Steve had been in danger. Could it be she cared for him more than he deserved?

Omar said softly: 'Your husband neither appreciates you nor loves you, so perhaps it is a pity there was no crocodile to dispose of him.'

'You mustn't suggest such an awful thing!' she flashed. 'I . . . I'd be inconsolable.' And she wondered if perhaps she would.

'But I would console you,' Omar said eagerly. 'Oh, my white rose, if only you were free!'

Noelle looked at him curiously, but her eyes dropped before the flame in his. He seemed to be an inflammable person. She did not believe his protestations, and she had no intention of embarking upon a liaison with him, which was what he wanted. But because her heart was sore because of Steve's treatment, she said provocatively:

'If I were free . . . what then?'

'I would take you away into the desert and make love to you as you should be loved.'

The idea of the romantic Arab sheik is long outdated, but Noelle felt a very faint stir of excitement at the passion in his voice.

'I . . . I've always found deserts fascinating,' she began, when the sound of voices caused her to pull away her hand, as Marcia and Steve burst into the lounge. She was scolding him vigorously and he was grinning like a naughty unrepentant schoolboy. His hair was wet and he was wrapped in a towelling robe.

'Such a crazy thing to do; Owen said he'd been very rude, so he deserved a ducking, and his mates could have got him out. But you . . .' She stopped abruptly as she caught sight of Noelle. 'Good morning, Mrs Prescott,' she said stiffly. 'Pity you weren't up on deck to stop Steve making a fool of himself.'

She had been sunbathing and wore a minute bikini, only a couple of straps, while dark glasses concealed her eyes. Steve's face froze, the boyish grin vanishing as he perceived who Noelle was with. No whit discomfited, Omar sprang to his feet.

'Coffee?' he suggested. 'You must need something after your . . . er . . . swim. This little lady feared you'd been eaten by crocodiles.'

'No, thanks, I've had a whisky,' Steve said shortly, with his eyes fixed on Noelle's face. 'Sorry to disappoint you, my love, but the crocs found me too tough. You'd have been a very rich widow.'

Noelle went red and then white. 'If that's meant to be a joke, it's in very poor taste,' she forced herself to say lightly, though the barb and gone home. Since she had told him she did not love him, he must have guessed her real motive. 'And Omar says there aren't any crocs now.'

Deliberately she used the Arab's first name, and saw Steve raise his brows.

'No one is formal on a ship,' she added, and glanced pointedly at Marcia's near-nakedness. Steve seemed to become aware of it.

'Hadn't you better put something on?' he said to her.

Marcia smiled lazily. 'Don't you like me like this?'

'In the right place,' Steve retorted, 'which isn't here. You'll give the old tabbies a fit.'

Noelle saw to her dismay that the Bates had come in. Mrs Bates uttered a small disapproving sound, but the Colonel put his eyeglass in his eye.

'I'm giving their husbands a treat,' Marcia announced shamelessly. She caught Omar's glance, which was more distasteful than admiring. 'Oh well, I'd better dress, I suppose, and you, darling,' she turned towards Steve, 'had better have a shower. I don't believe the Nile water is very healthy.'

Noelle caught her breath, recalling several unpleasant diseases that could be contracted in tropical waters.

'You shouldn't run such risks,' she said anxiously.

'No risk at all, and I was glad of a dip, since there's no pool on this ship. Get some clothes on, Marcia, British prestige abroad has sunk low enough without you bringing it down further.'

Marcia looked startled, and pouted, but she went out of the lounge, and after hesitating for a moment, Steve followed her.

Omar said softly: 'I understood the British practised monogamy.'

The colour ran up under Noelle's fair skin as she

caught the implication. She began to stammer—
Marcia was an old friend . . . it was coincidence that
she had come on this tour . . . her friends had let her
down . . . so naturally being old pals . . . Her voice
died away. Her excuses were weak and would not
deceive him any more than she believed in them
herself. Only loyalty to Steve had made her utter
them.

'That woman isn't fit to lick your sandals,' Omar
muttered.

Noelle felt she couldn't agree more, but she said
nothing. Marcia was expert at seduction and experienced in the ways of love; she could not compete
with her even if she tried to do so.

The Bates had gone back on deck and Noelle absently sat down again beside Omar. He leaned towards her, saying thickly:

'Oh, moon of my delight, why do you waste your
sweetness on such arid soil?'

His flowery phrase did not register, but she could
not mistake the lust in his eyes. He went on: 'Come
to me and you shall have anything and everything
for which you yearn. I am rich . . .'

'Oh, stop, please!' Noelle put her hands over her
ears, shrinking from his unconcealed passion. He was
avid to possess her cool northern beauty, but Steve
had given her all she could wish for in the way of
material gifts, including diamonds as well as the
pearls, but only Hugh had given her what was to
her infinitely more valuable—undemanding love.
When she had decided to marry Steve she had destroyed Hugh's photographs out of a sense of loyalty
to her new mate, but she had believed his image was

fixed in her memory for all time, only to discover it had become blurred. When she tried to recall his well loved features, another face interposed, hard aquiline profile, cynical smile and cold grey eyes; that of the man who had bought her and had now lost interest in her.

'I made a bargain with my husband and I must keep it,' she told Omar.

'Very dutiful,' he sneered, 'but you will come to me in the end.' For this spoilt princeling could not conceive that he would not obtain what he wanted eventually.

Noelle stood up. 'Thank you for the coffee,' she said formally. 'Please excuse me now, I must write some postcards.'

'Certainly.' Omar rose and bowed. He stood watching her graceful figure disappear with a confident smile on his full lips.

CHAPTER FIVE

NOELLE had no postcards, she had had no opportunity to buy some, but she remembered seeing a rack of them outside the office amidships. She wanted to send cards to Simon and her parents. There were plenty to choose from and stamps were procurable. There were pictures of the Pyramids, the Sphinx, and various temples, also desert scenes which recalled Omar. The man was not without attraction and she thought he would look splendid in native dress, the one-time popular sheik of romance. As she went towards her cabin she wove a fantasy in which she rode with him over sandy wastes towards an opulent tent set in an oasis surrounded by palms. He would be a fiery lover and perhaps could teach her how to respond to Steve. Then she shook herself and laughed at her folly. In any case she judged Omar was too sophisticated for such a simple setting. Though he had spoken of the desert, Paris or Nice would be more his mark, and he might become a nuisance if he became too importunate, though she could not believe he was really serious. Boredom and their exotic surroundings had much to answer for, but all would be changed when they reached Luxor and embarked upon the numerous excursions provided for them. It might happen that Marcia really did have friends coming to meet her there, and she, Noelle, would have the privilege of her husband's escort again. That would scotch Mr Omar ben Ahmed's encroachments, she thought with amusement. Steve would soon get rid of him. Meanwhile his attentions were flattering, and boosted her ego. She wondered what his real title was . . . Emir . . . Sheik . . . Khan? 'Mr' seemed incongruous.

Splashing, audible through the thin partition, indicated that Steve was in his own cabin taking the suggested shower. Instantly Omar was banished from her mind and her thoughts reverted to the incident of the early morning. Omar had mocked and Marcia had scolded, but it was probable that Steve's prompt action had saved the man's life, who, panic-stricken, might not have been able to grasp the life-belt. Noelle felt an urge to go to him and express her admiration for his courage and resource, but would he admit her? The door between them was locked in more senses than one.

An excuse occurred to her. The unfiltered Nile water presented a hazard, one that he was still risking. Taking a bottle of disinfectant from her case, she knocked upon the communicating door.

'Yes, what do you want?'

'I ... I've something for you. Something you need.'

Silence, and she feared Steve was not going to let her in. Then the key turned in the lock and he threw the door open. He was naked except for a towel wrapped around his middle, his bronzed body still dripping from the shower. It was that of a young man, flat stomach, long muscular thighs, the skin smooth over his powerful neck and shoulders. Only that touch of silver at his temples betrayed that he was no longer a boy, but a man in the prime of his health and strength. Noelle blinked, aware of a stirring of her senses. It was the first time she had seen him without his clothes in the full light of day, and she thought Michelangelo's David had nothing on him. He gave her a quizzical glance, as if he guessed her thoughts, and she held out the bottle.

'I thought you should use some of this.'

He took it from her and held it up to the light.

'To decontaminate me from the Nile water or Marcia's embraces?'

'Steve!' Noelle flinched. Had he no shame at all? The thought of Marcia in those strong arms gave her an acute stab of jealousy. 'Did you spend the night with her?' she asked bluntly.

He looked at her with a sneer.

'That's what you believe, isn't it?'

'All the evidence points to it.'

He scowled at the bottle. 'You judge me by the standards of that degenerate lot you worked with in the rag trade. Circumstantial evidence is never conclusive.'

Instantly Noelle took fire at this slur upon her former associates. How dared he pass judgment on them!

'If you're suggesting that Hugh . . .'

He dropped the bottle with an oath.

'Mention that name again and I'll strangle you!'

Noelle was delighted.

'Surely you can't be jealous of a dead man?'

'No,' he returned squashing her newborn hope. 'The trouble is he made you into a dead woman. Was his lovemaking so wonderful that you can't bear any other?'

About to tell him that Hugh had never made love to her in the sense he meant, Noelle checked herself. Marcia was still rankling. Why should she give him such an assurance when he continued to insult her by his connection with that woman? If she had not been there . . . but she was, and her red hair and green eyes would pursue them all the way up the Nile.

'Hugh,' she began, ignoring his threatening gesture as she spoke the name, 'was gentle and considerate, and I was the only woman in his life.'

Steve reached for his trousers, the towel slipping dangerously. Noelle modestly averted her head, but with a swift movement he concealed himself. Her action did not pass unnoticed.

'Such a modest little violet,' he jeered. 'One would think you were a virgin.'

Again Noelle was about to speak, but checked herself. Possibly a confession of her innocence would put him off. He had not the patience to initiate her, he preferred his women to be experienced.

'So the dress designer told you you were the only woman in his life,' Steve went on, his eyes glinting maliciously. 'And you believed him?'

'Of course. Hugh would never lie to me.'

Steve's thin lips curled satirically. 'My love, there are some subjects about which every man will lie to a woman.'

Out of his own mouth he was condemned.

'I'll remember that,' she returned.

Steve seemed to lose patience with her; he turned on her with a snarl.

'Get out of my room, unless . . .' He paused and a gleam came into his eyes. 'Unless you want to share my bed.'

'After what you've just confessed? Certainly not!'

'I haven't admitted a thing.'

'Oh yes, you have—that every man will lie to a woman. I know now how far I can trust your word in the face of circumstantial evidence.'

Steve's face set like stone as he said bitingly:

'Like all women you can twist words to suit your purpose. I'm quite indifferent to your opinion of me.'

He was rapidly becoming indifferent to her in every way, and she said despairingly: 'What a pity you married me!'

'Not at all. You'll look very decorative at my dining table when I entertain my friends.'

Along with the Crown Derby plate and silver cutlery, a possession brought out for special occasions. He met her stormy eyes with amusement in his, as he went on:

'You know I'm a collector of choice pieces, and that hair of yours will look well against the dark panelling of my dining room. I thought of that when I proposed to you.'

'Of all the cold-blooded . . .' she burst out.

'Come, come, my love, why such heat? You didn't marry me for love, but for material advantage, and that you've got in abundance.'

Noelle wished she could deny it, but she had accepted him for the sake of her parents and Simon. It came to her then that she wanted to be much more to Steve than the mere figurehead he had suggested, but they had started off on the wrong foot, and now Marcia had come to widen the rift.

The amusement died out of Steve's face and he said sternly:

'But watch your step with that Arab type, he's only got one use for a woman, as you'll soon find out.'

At the end of her endurance she flung at him:

'Then you and he are two of the same sort!'

Steve smiled unpleasantly.

'That being so, you'd better get out of my room.'

Noelle fled, pursued by his mocking laughter. She heard the key grate in the lock as he closed the door behind her.

The day before the *Serapis* was due to arrive in Luxor was one of hectic activity. The Excursion Manager had come aboard and everyone was arranging their trips. They were all rather bored with the long journey, for though the ship had passed several towns on her way up the Nile, she had not put in to them. They were to be visited on her return journey, when it was hoped they would prove an attraction to deter passengers returning by air. Noelle was spending most of her time with the Bates, for though she met Steve at meals, he had become immersed in plans for a take-over, and shut himself in his cabin amid a pile of papers, except when he was trying to send radiograms, and upsetting the crew with impossible demands. At least he was not with Marcia, who when he did appear greeted him with reproaches. Why must he work on a holiday? He replied tersely that something had blown up which required intricate calculations, which he must complete before they reached Luxor and a more efficient communication system. Marcia turned her attention to Omar, to Noelle's chagrin, for in spite of his derogatory remarks about the redhead, he did not seem averse to her company. For all that she was often conscious of his eyes fixed upon her speculatively if she happened to be in his vicinity, though he did not approach her, and Noelle wondered if Steve had warned him off.

The Bates were too tactful to ask questions, but Noelle could see they were a little puzzled by their relationships. They dubbed Marcia an adventuress and were sorry for Noelle, whose husband neglected her. They all wanted to go to the Valley of the Kings, and the Colonel asked her if she would like to go with them. Not knowing what Steve's plans were, and whether they included Marcia, she said she would be glad to do so if her husband agreed. He did not. He told her brusquely he had made arrangements for her entertainment, adding disagreeably:

'Are you trying to annex that old hasbeen now?'

Noelle stared at him in astonishment. Surely he could not disapprove of the Colonel?

'He's a very nice gentleman,' she said, 'and his wife's a dear. Since you leave me to my own devices, I have to talk to someone.'

'I don't flatter myself you're pining for my company,' he retorted. He seemed tired and irritated.

Stung, she returned. 'Hardly that, but you should give me some of it, for appearances' sake.'

'Quite unnecessary.' He regarded her moodily. 'By now both crew and passengers will know that we sleep apart.'

Including, of course, Marcia and Omar. Noelle sighed and turned away. Marcia must be filling his needs and he no longer desired her—the thought was bitter gall, but she would make no advance while the other woman was in possession, she could not bear to share him. Steve went back to his cabin and his work, while she went to tell Colonel Bates she must refuse his kind invitation.

The next day the *Serapis* reached Luxor. The town is situated on a flood plain of the Nile which covers a wide area. It is built on the site of the eighteenth-dynasty ancient capital of Thebes, of which nothing remains except its rich heritage of temple ruins. In the old days there were two cities, the east bank one with its palaces and gardens and across the Nile the

City of the Dead. Because the Ancient Egyptians were much preoccupied with death the latter had been of unsurpassed splendour. The kings were buried in rock tombs, burrowed deep into the Theban Hills in a vain attempt to conceal them from grave robbers. These had operated often only a generation or so after the funeral, abetted by corruption in high places. The discovery of Tutankhamen's tomb, with all its rich treasures, gave some idea of the immense value of the offerings entombed with the great Pharaohs, for Tutankhamen was only a minor king and not much more than a boy when he died. The mind boggles to imagine the wealth that would have surrounded a ruler like Rameses the Second. It provided a temptation too great to be resisted.

As the actual burying places had to be hidden, the dead were honoured by large mortuary temples built along the western bank. The attendant priests and their servants, the architects, builders and masons engaged upon performing services for the dear departed and erecting new buildings were housed in this vast necropolis, and many of the temples they were engaged upon are still standing. The biggest of them all, the huge temple erected by Amenhotep the Third, who was responsible for most of the building in Thebes, is demolished, except for the Colossi of Memnon, the great stone statues of the Pharaoh himself, which still stand at what was once the entrance to it. With the dawn of the Christian era the city had dwindled to a mere village, but eventually the modern city of Luxor came into being, and was now a flourishing tourist centre, with hotels, an airport and other Western amenities. It occupies only a small portion of the site of the original mighty town.

The *Serapis* arrived at Luxor as she had departed from Cairo, in the glory of the sunset. Noelle stood on the little deck watching the pageant of the sun's departing below the Theban Hills, heedless of the bustle below her of passengers coming and going. She was wondering what Steve's plans were for the morrow.

To her surprise, he came out to join her, and as they stood side by side at the rail, he said softly:

'Osiris returning to his nether kingdom. He was identified with the sun, you know, and Isis with the moon.'

'I thought Amon-re was the god of Thebes.'

'So you know that? Yes, Amon-re was the supreme god, like Zeus in Greek mythology, but Osiris was important too.'

'Who was destroyed by Set the evil one and the sorrowing Isis collected his remains. Her tears caused the Nile to flood and bring fertility to the land.'

'She must have wept prodigiously. Would you have wept if I'd succumbed to . . . the crocodile that morning?'

Noelle stared at his dim profile beside her in amazement. His eyes were fixed on the distant hills and his voice was gentle. She did not know him in this mood.

'Not enough to flood the Nile,' she returned, 'but what's got into you, Steve? You weren't in any real danger, and' . . . her slight bosom swelled, 'you taunted me with being a rich widow.' She had not forgiven him for that.

'Which of course would have been an enormous consolation.'

Now he was jeering, a more familiar Steve.

'No,' she said quietly, 'I don't think wealth is all that important.'

'Really? Then why on earth did you marry me?'

'Because my life was so empty, and my parents were set on it. Besides, you were very persistent.'

'Unwisely so.'

Noelle went cold. So he was regretting their marriage. Was he thinking Marcia's sophistication was more suited to the position of his wife? She had acted as hostess for him before, and red hair would look as striking against his dining room panelling as her own pale blonde locks. The shock those two words had given her surprised her. Could it be possible she had fallen in love with her husband, and in so short a time? It was an unwelcome thought, because Steve despised love; he had said with satisfaction that he had learned to live without it. If she had been more receptive on that fatal night, her position might have been more secure, but all he had wanted then was physical satisfaction, which he had since found elsewhere. Love, she knew, meant so much more, and it was painful to her to realise she could love again after Hugh, and a man like Steve Prescott, for she doubted if any woman could come close to him; in his heart he despised her sex.

The glow from the sunset threw his face into strong relief, the harsh lean planes of cheek and chin, the dark bar of his eyebrows, and the surprisingly long lashes which should have softened the hardness of his eyes, but never did. His head was set proudly upon his broad shoulders, which made him appear more arrogant than he actually was. He was still gazing at the last red rim of the sun, disappearing behind the hills, and his mouth had an unusually gentle curve.

She said firmly: 'It's done now.'

'What's done can always be undone.'

Her heart jolted, almost with fear. He had said once that what he had he would hold and the words had seemed to her a threat of permanent bondage. But even Steve could change his mind. Noelle had always understood an unconsummated marriage could be annulled without much difficulty. Was that what he had in mind? Unconsciously she had begun to lean on him, for she was not the independent type of woman, and when she had worked at Forbes Fashions she had relied upon Hugh throughout her employment there. His demise had meant not only the loss of her lover but her anchor and bulwark. Without him she had felt adrift and that was partly why she had accepted Steve. The strident advocates of women's rights would have told her she had a slave mentality, and she would have retorted that two bosses did not make for a harmonious home life. She was perfectly willing to be guided by her husband if he could be persuaded to do the guiding, but at the moment it looked as though their semi-detached existence might deteriorate into total separation. The prospect of a return to single life filled her with dismay, and not only that, she had been shocked into the realisation that she wanted Steve, and desired passionately to remove the barrier that had sprung up between them, and drive the marauding Marcia off her preserves.

How could she break down Steve's indifferent façade? Convince him that she would welcome his embrace? But she was not quite certain of her own feelings, though the memory of their wedding night caused an excited flutter in her stomach when she envisioned a repetition. The hot Egyptian sun engendered eroticism, but she had not quite broken through her inhibitions. She needed his encouragement.

She looked at him wistfully. In the fading light he was a tall, dim shape, dominating but unapproachable. He had not liked Omar's attentions to her, and it flashed into her mind that there she had a weapon with which she could revive his interest in her. He was jealous of his possessions, and the male in him, and he was very male, would resent a rival. Only dimly conscious of the primitive forces within both herself and him with which she was playing, Noelle said provocatively:

'If you're thinking of walking out on me I can always fall back on our Arabian prince.'

'You'd be a damned fool if you did,' Steve told her brusquely, which was not the reaction for which she had hoped. 'I can't think what you see in that layabout.'

Then the full significance of her words seemed to hit him, and he grasped her shoulders painfully. 'What have you and he been up to?'

'Nothing . . . as yet.'

His touch set her vibrating like a harp in the wind. So this was love, something far more physical than she had ever experienced with Hugh, and far more overwhelming. Forcing herself to speak lightly, she went on:

'He's offered to show me the desert. It might be rather . . . thrilling.'

'Is that what you want? A thrill?' His hands dropped from her shoulders to close over her back. He was drawing her nearer to his broad chest. Noelle did feel a thrill, of excitement, and her lips parted in anticipation of his kiss. All was not lost if she could arouse desire in him, but almost immediately he dropped his arms.

'I was forgetting, I don't thrill you . . . only revolt you.'

A whiplash could not have hurt her more than his withdrawal. Her half aroused senses recoiled like a released spring.

'Oh, Steve,' she cried reproachfully, 'it's not like that at all!'

The sun had gone and darkness was rushing over the land with the speed night descended in that latitude. She could not distinguish his features, but his voice held the familiar gibe when he spoke:

'Isn't it? Don't try to perjure yourself, my love, out of a sense of wifely duty. I know what your true feelings are, and I've come to dislike bought kisses.'

'You've had plenty of them,' she said bitterly struggling to control her chaotic emotions. She was not sure if she loved or hated him.

'Exactly, and they've become sour.'

Noelle sought for words to convince him that he was mistaken about her attitude towards him, but she was too confused by her changed feelings to think coherently. There was silence between them, while her heart knocked against her ribs with such violence that she thought Steve must be able to hear it. Lights came on all over the ship; it had been dressed overall in coloured bulbs to celebrate their arrival. She saw Steve was standing apart from her gazing towards the shore, seeming no more moved by her presence than if she had been a dummy.

He turned his head, and said casually, as if nothing had passed between them:

'I'm afraid I must leave you this evening. I've got to try to contact London and it may take a long time.'

That tiresome take-over that was absorbing him. Noelle was disappointed; she had hoped he would suggest dinner at the hotel which would be a change from meals on board, but she knew business was paramount with him, and she must accept it. She only prayed he was not using it as an excuse to avoid her company.

'That's all right with me,' she said listlessly.

'I've ascertained your friends the Bates are dining on the ship. I've asked them to look after you.'

'How very thoughtful of you,' she said sarcastically, wondering if he had appointed the elderly couple as guardians to prevent her slipping off with Omar, but he had not seemed to be very put out about her acquaintanceship with the Arab, and Omar would have gone ashore.

'Don't sit up late,' he went on. 'We have to make an early start tomorrow, so you'll need your sleep. I'm taking you to the Valley of the Kings.'

'Alone?' she asked doubtfully, fearing Marcia would be going with them.

'Quite alone, with a specially hired guide. Did

you want your desiccated Colonel to be included in the party?'

'Of course not.' Noelle's face was radiant. Perhaps all her fears were groundless. Steve had arranged this expedition to please her and she would be alone with him all day. Perhaps it would be possible to come to a better understanding with him away from Marcia's pervasive influence.

'Good. I'll see you in the morning, then. Wear trousers, they're the best garments for scrambling about in tombs. So long.'

He went into his cabin to collect his briefcase, and Noelle ran down to the next deck and along the balcony until she reached a spot overlooking the gangway. Passengers were going ashore in twos and threes, chattering gaily. Few wanted to stay on the ship now they had a chance to stretch their legs. Noelle would have liked to join them, but she knew it would be foolish to wander about alone at night in a strange city. Presently she saw what she had come for. Steve came striding out of the ship on to the gangway. He had changed his blazer for a beige linen jacket and carried his case. He looked every inch the purposeful executive. Women, Noelle thought sadly, were only a very minor distraction to him. The sailors at the foot of the gangway saluted and Noelle caught a glimpse of his smiling face, as he exchanged some quip with them. For all his authoritative air, Steve had the common touch.

Noelle drew a long breath as she watched his tall, lean figure disappear into the miscellaneous crowd on the quayside. The inevitable street vendors were there with their monotonous chant—'Only one . . .

two . . . three . . . dollars,' as the case might be. A man among men, she thought, and wondered that she could have been so blind to his worth. He had told her once that she should be proud that he had chosen to marry her, and for the first time she was. He was totally different from Hugh, who had been almost feminine in his intuitions. She could not expect the same rapport from Steve, who was so very masculine. She did not want it, she was feminine enough to be willing to submit to his mastery. Somehow she must detach him from Marcia and make her marriage work.

As if on cue, Marcia appeared on the gangway, wearing a long evening dress. The lights turned her red head to fire, and jewels gleamed at her throat and ears. A man and a woman came to greet her, people Noelle had never seen before, thereby confirming that she had spoken the truth when she said her friends were meeting her at Luxor. Noelle felt guilty that she had doubted her . . . and Steve.

Marcia's high shrill voice floated up to her.

'So lovely to see you! Steve will meet us at the Luxor Hotel. He had to go on ahead.'

So that was why Steve was going to be late back, if he returned at all. Noelle smiled bitterly. The expedition on the morrow was a sop offered to a deserted wife to square his conscience for leaving her tonight. All too probably, at the last moment, she would find that Marcia and her friends had been included in the excursion, when she had used her persuasions on him. Not that he would need much persuading. Noelle stared blindly at the lights of the town. If Steve had not exactly lied to her, he had done so by implication. He had no scruples about lying to a woman.

She felt a touch on her shoulder and turning, found Omar ben Ahmed beside her. She stared at him a little blankly, for she had been certain that he would have gone ashore. He was smiling insinuatingly, and she hoped he had not been there to hear Marcia's words.

'Will you come and have dinner with me?' he asked. 'I know a very nice place in Luxor right off the tourist track. It will be more amusing than staying here on your own.'

CHAPTER SIX

NOELLE's first impulse was to accept, but her years as a model had taught her caution. Men had often propositioned her with invitations to private residences, and Omar's intentions were probably similar to what theirs had been. Much as she would have liked to spite Steve by going out with him, and possibly encountering Steve and Marcia in the Arab's company, she knew it would be extremely unwise. So she thanked him for his kind thought and told him she would not be alone as she had promised to dine with the Bates.

Omar's dark brows went up. 'That old couple! I thought the ladies of the West had dispensed with chaperones.'

'It's not that at all,' she said quickly, though she

had a shrewd idea that that had been Steve's intention. Her elderly friends presented no threat to her integrity. Though he preferred Marcia's company to hers, he would not permit any sideslipping upon her part, as he had told her. Caesar's wife must be beyond reproach, though Caesar himself might . . . and did . . . stray.

'I like the Bates and I can't disappoint them.'

To her surprise he suggested: 'In that case perhaps they would come with you' He gave her a sly glance. 'The jealous husband could not then disapprove. My friend Suleiman has a very original house here, which, as he is away, he has placed at my disposal, and I wish very much for you to see it. Your friends too will enjoy a change. The Colonel has been in the East, he will appreciate it.'

Noelle still hesitated, though she wanted very much to go. Steve, she felt sure, would be angry, but she did not owe him any consideration after the way he had treated her.

'It's wonderful of you to offer, but . . .'

'Come, we will go and ask them,' Omar interrupted, and led the way into the ship. If the Bates refused, that would settle it, and she did not expect they would accept.

Colonel Bates was an Anglophile, he had no use for foreigners, be they princes or stevedores, and he looked suspiciously at Omar ben Ahmed, when he gave his invitation.

'We had arranged to dine on the ship,' he began stiffly, when he caught Noelle's appealing glance and his wife's wistful expression. They had scraped up enough money for this Nile trip which they con-

sidered to be a last fling before they settled down to
retirement, but they had nothing to spare for extras.
It would be a treat for Mary, and her husband had
left that nice little Mrs Prescott high and dry when
he went ashore bent upon his own diversions. She
was a deuced pretty woman and it was a shame the
way he neglected her. He changed his tone.

'Well, it's very civil of you, I'm sure, and the ladies
will enjoy an outing.'

Mary Bates, all of a flutter, said she must change
her dress, and Noelle did likewise. They reappeared,
Noelle in blue nylon draped over a silk underslip,
Mrs Bates in black lace. The Colonel had been
already wearing his dinner jacket.

It was only when they were seated in the hired
car that Omar told them that they were not going
to the Luxor Hotel, for Noelle had left it to him to
tell them. The Colonel looked doubtful.

'That all right by you, Mrs Prescott?'

He had never got round to using her first name,
though his wife did.

'Oh yes, Mr ben Ahmed says it's unique, and
I'm longing to see it.'

The old gentleman looked a little uneasy, and
muttered something about hoping that the wog
wasn't up to some monkey trick, which Omar, seated
beside the chauffeur, luckily did not hear, and Mary
hurriedly hushed him. She was full of enthusiasm
for such an unexpected pleasure. Omar told them:

'I am most grateful for your honoured company.
I could not have taken Mrs Prescott alone, of course,
and I very much wanted to show her Suleiman's
house. You will all be most impressed.'

From the outside the place was nothing remarkable, a square white building, its high walls windowless, but inside it was fabulous.

The ground floor rooms all opened on to a square courtyard in the centre of the building, in the middle of which was a stone basin with a fountain. The basin was filled with blue lotus lilies and fragrant bushes in pots filled the air with sweetness. Omar had told them his friend was eccentric and crazy about Ancient Egypt; the room they were shown into bore this out.

It was open on one side to the courtyard, but the other three lofty walls were covered with paintings copied from those in the royal tombs. They depicted various activities of Egyptian life, ploughing, sowing, hunting and fowling. In the centre of each wall was a long oval shaped like a cartouche, enclosing the effigy of a god. There was Amon-re, with his tall feathered headdress, Osiris wearing the double crown of Upper and Lower Egypt, which Noelle privately thought looked like an urn stuck in a saucepan, and the hawk-headed Horus, son of Isis.

Across the domed ceiling was a huge female figure, with her feet on the top of one wall, her head on the opposite one—Nut, the goddess of the sky. The doorway into the house was between two pillars, engraved with hieroglyphics, their capitals decorated with papyrus plant buds, as are the ones in the colonnade of the temple at Luxor. The furniture, also copied from that found in the tombs, comprised chairs and tables, ornately carved and inset with gold. The couch was an Egyptian bed, with cow-shaped ends, their heads forming the arms, and between their horns, the moon disc, emblem of Hathor, goddess of love.

The Colonel stared at it all with astonishment.

'We hardly need to go sightseeing, Mary,' he exclaimed. 'The whole of Egypt is here.'

'In miniature,' said Omar, indicating they should be seated. 'Wine?' He clapped his hands and a servant ran in salaaming. 'Or do you prefer spirits?' He knew the Colonel liked whisky.

Colonel Bates looked surprised. 'Spirits? Here?'

'Suleiman's cellar is stocked to please every visitor, though he and I abstain.' Omar caught Noelle's eye. 'At least when I'm on Arab soil.'

When they had all been served, Noelle and Mary choosing innocuous tomato juice, Omar begged to be excused for a moment. They sat in silence overwhelmed by their surroundings, then the Colonel said, à propos the absent Suleiman:

'Crazy fellow, but by Jove, he must have some cash!'

Omar returned wearing Arab dress.

'It is,' he explained, 'so much more comfortable.'

The long kaftan with its jewelled belt, flowing cloak and striped, corded headdress, became him. The garb was far more romantic than his Western clothes, and Noelle felt sure he knew it.

Mary Bates said, 'Ah, now you're in the picture. How fine you look!'

Omar smiled, his white even teeth splitting his brown face which seemed darker against his robes.

'Not quite. This is Arab dress, not Egyptian. Their costume was a little too scanty for entertaining a lady like yourself. Now let us dine.'

They were served Eastern food, fish soup followed by roasted lamb and rice, kebabs, and couscous, the staple food of the Bedouin, which was a preparation of semolina, finally a sweet comprised of honey and nuts. They drank glasses of mint tea, which Omar prepared for them himself. Soft-footed servants in djellabas and turbans waited on them. When these had removed the debris of the feast, they sat replete listening to native musicians out in the courtyard, playing on reed pipes. Their host produced Turkish cigarettes and cigars, and Noelle, who was not a smoker, tried one of the gold-banded oval Turks, which was much too strong and made her cough.

At length Colonel Bates roused himself and said:

'You've entertained us royally, my boy, but it's time we went back to the ship. It must be very late.'

'As you wish. The bathroom is through the door, on your left. You will find modern plumbing.'

Both the Colonel and his wife availed themselves of this invitation, and Omar turned to Noelle.

'I will send them back with the chauffeur, but you, my heart's delight, will stay, will you not? This shall be a night to remember.'

He stood close beside her, and he smelt of musk and sandalwood; his dark eyes were swimming and his low voice shook with passion.

Noelle felt an unwilling response. Her sexuality, which had started to awaken under Steve's guidance, was stirred by his proximity, his handsome presence and his obvious desire. This evening, with its voluptuous setting, had been planned to bring about her seduction. Unconsciously she swayed towards him, and he laid a burning hand on her bare arm.

'Allah be praised! You will give yourself at last!'

The invocation of an unfamiliar god broke the spell and restored her to sanity. Gently she removed his hand.

'Omar, I'm sorry, I can't. I have a husband.'

'Who prefers another woman. He is with her now.'

Noelle was very much afraid he was.

'I know, but all the same, I'm married to him and I . . . I love him.'

There, it was out, and with the words the last of her uncertainty died. All unawares Steve had stolen her heart, and the memory of Hugh no longer stood between them. Not that he had done anything to win her love—or was she being unfair? He had spared her on their wedding night, when he had perceived her fear, and he had brought her to Egypt because he had been told it was her wish. The fault for their estrangement lay with her, but now she was sure of her own feelings, there must be a way to win him back. Absorbed in the realisation of her newborn love, she had forgotten the man beside her, until Omar touched her shoulder. She started out of her dream and said again:

'I'm so sorry. I'm afraid you've taken all this trouble for nothing.'

'But you are here,' he told her softly. 'I will not let you go.'

Noelle looked at him uncertainly.

'You can't keep me here against my will.'

'Can I not? Oh, Noelle, you are teasing me, as women do—you want to stay, and it will be quite easy. The servants will conduct your friends to the car, they will say that you will follow, but I am showing you my friend's collection of scarabs.' (A variation on etchings, she thought drily.) 'The old one is a man of the world, he will understand why you came. You will stay?'

A part of her did want to surrender, for it was sweet and flattering to be desired, with Hugh gone and Steve indifferent, but she could not betray her love.

'It's impossible,' she said firmly. 'The Bates will tell Steve where I am; he'll be angry.'

'If he asks, but I do not think that one will return tonight.'

So he had overheard Marcia's words, and shared her suspicions. Noelle thought of the empty cabin next her own, the locked door, and her eyes met Omar's eager gaze. Here was someone who did want her.

There was a sudden commotion outside, and a servant rushed in and threw himself at Omar's feet.

'Pardon, *effendi*, pardon, I could not keep him out.'

Omar looked furious, he kicked the man's prostrate body.

'Son of a bitch, camel's dung!' He relapsed into angry Arabic, while the unfortunate man cringed before him. Noelle looked towards the door, thinking now was her chance to escape, and saw Steve standing on the threshold. With a glad cry she ran towards him, but he pushed her aside.

'A most edifying scene,' he drawled, 'but I gather I'm not too late.'

'How in Shaitan's name did you get here?' Omar snarled.

'In a car, of course. One of the crew saw you go

off with my wife, and everyone in Luxor knows of
your connection with the owner of this house. When
I found you weren't at the hotel, I guessed you'd
brought her here.'

'The Bates came with me,' Noelle told him
defensively.

'Indeed? But I don't see them here. You and this
... this scum were enjoying a tête-à-tête, a prelude
to the bedroom act, I assume.'

'They *are* here,' Noelle cried desperately, hoping
they had not gone, and then to her relief the Colonel
appeared in the doorway behind Steve.

'Extraordinary thing, Mrs Prescott,' he began, as
Steve stood aside to allow him to enter. 'The butler,
major-domo, whatever he is, was trying to shoo us
away without you.'

His faded blue eyes blinked at Noelle anxiously.
As Omar said, he was sophisticated enough to suspect that Omar's lavish hospitality had an ulterior
motive, but he couldn't believe she had encouraged
him, she wasn't that sort. 'But I understand now,'
he went on with obvious relief. 'The fellow didn't
explain that you were waiting for your husband to
collect you.'

There was an uneasy pause, and Noelle moistened
her lips with the tip of her tongue. Steve and Omar
were eyeing each other like matadors watching a
bull, each waiting for the other's next move. To her
horror she saw Omar's hand move towards the
dagger he wore in his belt, a pretty ornament, but
deadly for all that. She braced herself to spring between them—better she was stabbed than Steve, who
was here as a result of her folly, for she had known

subconsciously all along that some sinister motive lay behind the Arab's lavish hospitality.

Then Mary Bates came into the room, bringing with her a breath of normality, she was such an ordinary sane figure in her slightly shabby black lace with her air of respectability.

She went up to Omar with her hand outstretched, saying:

'Thank you, thank you a hundred times, Mr ben Ahmed, for a truly wonderful evening. It's something I'll never forget. You've been too kind. Harry, I'm told the car is waiting, and I suppose Noelle is going back with her husband.'

'She is,' Steve said grimly.

Her gentle gush had broken the tension. Omar touched her fingertips and smiled wryly.

'My pleasure, dear lady.' He threw Noelle an enigmatical look and shrugged his shoulders. '*Insh'allah*,' he added resignedly, accepting with oriental fatalism the failure of his hopes.

The Colonel, looking a little stern, tendered his thanks, but Steve, taking hold of Noelle's arm, hauled her out of the room without giving her a chance to speak. He pushed her without ceremony into the back of the hired car and got in beside her.

'Back to the *Serapis*,' he ordered the chauffeur, and relapsed into ominous silence.

Noelle said nervously: 'It was so dull on the ship, and I thought it would be all right to accept his invitation as he asked the Bates too.'

'Whom he was about to dispose of.'

'But I wouldn't have stayed on alone.'

'Wouldn't you?'

'No.'

Silence again. She knew he didn't believe her.

'Anyway, you were with Marcia,' she flung at him.

'I was not.'

'She told her friends she was expecting you.'

'Marcia's expectations aren't always fulfilled.'

There was such a wealth of meaning in his voice, that Noelle was impressed. Had she been leaping to conclusions and Steve had not been sleeping with the amorous redhead? He had told her he had not been with her tonight, and certainly he had returned much earlier than she had expected. She felt a lift of her spirits, perhaps Marcia was not the threat she had feared, but they sank again as she remembered what Steve had said about masculine deceit. He would not scruple to lie about Marcia if it suited him.

They reached the ship, and throwing some money to the chauffeur, he followed her on board. On the second deck, she paused. This was where the Bates' cabin was situated.

'They may have got back first, and I'd like to say goodnight to them.'

'Don't try to procrastinate,' he told her sternly. 'You've made enough use of them for one night. Go on up to your cabin. I'm going to punish you for your disgraceful behaviour.'

'But I haven't done anything . . .'

'No, because I arrived in time.' With a hand on her back he pushed her up the last flight of stairs. 'You've been hankering after that louse ever since we came aboard. The moment my back is turned you rush to him.'

Noelle stumbled on to their own deck, and turned to face him as they reached her cabin door. Was he going to beat her . . . or what?

'He was kind, and you neglected me,' she said reproachfully.

'By your own wish, but you're not going to be neglected tonight. You may call me a brute and a monster, but I've indulged you too long. You're my wife, and you're going to know it!'

He seemed to fill her little cabin, and she shrank back against the wall in terror. How had she ever imagined she could love this cruel beast? For he was not going to take her because he loved her, or even desired her, but to punish her for supposed unfaithfulness. Unjust, unfair—she had rejected Omar for his sake and he wouldn't even listen to her. He was consumed with icy rage.

He went on: 'I haven't kept my hands off you so you can play games with the first man who takes your fancy, you with your touch-me-not airs and your pretended devotion to a dead man's memory. You're a hypocrite and a cheat! I should have known a mannequin is little better than a tart. You'll do your duty tonight, though it kills you. Get your clothes off.'

He threw off his jacket, and unfastened his shirt. Noelle did not move, and naked except for his underpants, Steve came to her, stripping her pretty nylon dress from her shoulders, tearing it beyond repair. Slip and bra followed it, and seizing her round the waist, he flung her down upon the narrow bed.

'Come, my love,' he mocked her. 'Show me some of the pretty tricks your couture lover taught you. If you can tolerate Omar's caresses, you can't be as cold as you pretended to be.'

Noelle stared up at him with agonised eyes.

'Steve, please listen! This could be so different if only you . . .'

'Shut up!'

He came down on her then, not caring how much he hurt her, not troubling to seek to arouse her with any love-play. She was stifled, crushed . . . there was pain. Steve gave a startled exclamation, but he had gone too far to draw back. Her mind blacked out as she was submerged in a flood of burning sensation.

She became aware that she was alone, there was a sound of running water, and the door between their cabins was ajar. Steve came back into hers wearing a towelling robe. She turned on her side away from him, drawing up her knees, trying to conceal her body in her streaming hair.

'No,' she whispered faintly, for she could endure no more.

He stared down at her white figure which looked as fragile as a broken flower.

'God forgive me,' he said huskily. 'I'd no idea you were still a virgin.'

'But . . . didn't you expect . . .?' Her voice was a mere thread.

'No. You'd been a model, and virgins are rare anyway, nowadays. Then there was that fellow . . . wasn't he your lover?'

She shook her head. 'We . . . waited . . .'

'I must have hurt you.'

'You were brutal.'

He seemed at a loss to know what to say; contrition

was not his strong point. Noelle raised herself and slid off the bed.

'I want a shower.'

She stood a long time under the spray, the warm water cleansing and reviving her. She noticed dark marks on her white skin. She bruised all too easily, but her mind was numb, and all she desired now was to sleep. Finally wrapping herself in a towel, she went back into the cabin.

Her bed had been remade with clean linen, and the door into Steve's was still ajar. Vaguely she wondered how he had found service so late at night. She sank down on the bed and closed her eyes. Then she opened them in alarm. Steve was standing over her.

'I'm not going to touch you,' he said gently, 'but why, oh, why did you encourage that swine? You're not so innocent you didn't know what he was after.'

Because of you and Marcia—but she did not say it. Instead she gave a long sigh and closed her eyes again. Steve drew up the sheet and covered her.

'Tomorrow,' he told her, 'we're flying back to London.'

Her eyes half opened, a line of blue between white lids.

'Oh, why?'

'Business. I must return, my presence is needed. I'm sorry to break off our . . . er . . . holiday, but it's not been a great success, has it?'

Noelle did not answer that, instead she murmured vaguely:

'Then we shan't see the Valley of the Kings.'

Steve hesitated. He had meant to cancel that expedition, but if she really wanted to go, he felt he owed her some reparation for his violence.

'The flight isn't until the evening, we'd have time for that.'

She was indifferent whether they went or not, but she didn't want to spend the day on the ship, Marcia and Omar might still be there. She said faintly:

'That would be nice.'

Steve stood looking down at her with a worried frown. Then to her astonishment, he stooped and tenderly kissed her brow.

'Goodnight, my love,' he said gently.

Then he had gone, and she thought she must have been already asleep and dreamed it. Voice and gesture were so unlike him. But he left the door between their cabins standing open.

CHAPTER SEVEN

NOELLE was awakened by the stewardess bringing in her breakfast, and looking at her watch she saw it was much earlier than usual. Of course, the expedition to the Valley of the Kings! Steve must have ordered it yesterday when he was making arrangements, before . . .

Noelle settle herself back against her pillows, distastefully eyeing the rolls and butter. The coffee she drank eagerly, but felt no wish for food. The events of the previous night filtered back to her with painful clarity. She had been amazed to discover Steve had believe she had lived with Hugh, though she supposed it was not surprising, so many girls nowadays embarked upon a trial period before finally binding themselves. To Steve, with his materialistic outlook, love meant consummation, and she had told him she loved Hugh and was going to marry him. He had thought none of the worse of her for that, regarding her as some sort of widow, but it explained his snide remarks about her dead lover, and his resentment of her apparent coldness towards himself.

A woman who had been aroused did not meet sex with virginal shrinking as she had done. She had sustained a physical shock from his assault upon her. The dawning love she had confessed to Omar was as bruised as her body. It was as if a late-flowering rose, opening delicate petals to the rays of the sun, had met the sharp nip of frost before it could bloom. Whether it would recover or wither away, she could not decide, for her feelings towards her husband were in a state of chaos—love and hate, repulsion and attraction warred for supremacy, only that last kiss offered balm to her hurt susceptibilities, but that she was sure she had dreamed, for neither by word nor look had Steve ever shown her any tenderness, and the door between their cabins was shut.

It flashed into her mind that he could not now annul their marriage, and again she was not certain if she were glad or sorry. Yesterday she would have been relieved, but this morning? It all depended upon how he treated her henceforth. If he were suitably contrite . . . Steve contrite? She nearly laughed. That would be the day! She didn't suppose he would appear any different from usual, but what about tonight? Then she recollected that they would be leaving, and the night would be spent over two thousand feet up in the air. No problem there, and thank God they would have left Omar and Marcia behind.

Meanwhile she must get up and get ready for this excursion, upon which she did not want to go, for she felt languid and would prefer to rest, but she could not think up an excuse that did not sound feeble, and Steve would imagine she was sulking because he had asserted his rights. And they were his rights, she must remember that, the payment for all he had given her. He had not cancelled the arrangements, being under the impression that she wanted this last trip, he might even have meant it as a way of making amends for his brutality, but it was hardly adequate.

She dressed in cream-coloured slacks and an amber shirt, as she combed her hair she noticed a mark on her neck. She went hot as she realised what it was. Selecting a chiffon scarf, she draped it about her neck to conceal it. The linen hat and dark glasses completed her toilet. Neither were becoming, but she had learned to respect the Egyptian sun.

When she went out on deck she found Steve waiting for her, standing looking over the rail. He too was wearing trousers and a linen coat, but instead of the Arab headdress—Arab was a dirty word to him after last night—a panama hat. As he rarely wore one, it made him look unfamiliar, so that Noelle hesitated, a slim, boyish figure standing half in sun and half in shade, but there was no mistaking that tall, lean body that had embraced her so savagely last night, and as he turned to look at her, the blood ran up under her thin skin, making her blush fierily.

'Hello, you're in good time.'

'You told me to be,' she said dully, vaguely disappointed by this casual greeting, though she did not know what else she had expected. Her heart was beating rapidly, a sign that physically she was reacting to his presence, however resentful her mind might be. He came towards her.

'What have you got round your neck?'

'Oh, just a scarf.'

'You won't need that.' He whisked it away and saw what she had sought to hide. Again Noelle blushed and hung her head.

Steve touched it with the tip of one finger.

'A love bite,' he said softly.

'I wouldn't call it that,' she returned disdainfully. 'The mark of the beast would be more accurate.'

He looked at her searchingly, but she turned her head away, and he sighed.

'Come on, we'd better get moving.'

Noelle pushed the scarf into the neck of her shirt and preceded him down the companionway. They had reached the lowest promenade and were proceeding towards the gangway, when there was a patter of slippered feet behind them, and an urgent voice called:

'Steve! Wait!'

Marcia had evidently dashed out of her cabin when she saw them go by. She had pulled on a wrap over her pyjamas, but she had not done her face. The morning light made her look haggard, and under the boudoir cap on her head she was wearing curlers.

'Where did you get to last night?' she asked reproachfully. 'I wanted you to meet my friends.'

'Sorry about that, but I had another appointment,' he returned smoothly. 'Something very urgent cropped up.'

His eyes flickered towards Noelle, who tried not to look conscious.

'Oh? Was someone playing truant?'

Noelle was sure then that Marcia had known of Omar's invitation, had probably connived at it, and it was part of the plan to lure Steve to the hotel so he would not miss her. She had seen them hobnobbing together. She waited anxiously for Steve's reply.

His face was bland, as he replied:

'What an odd idea! Who would want to do that?'

'Oh, I get these . . . hunches,' Marcia shrugged. 'It seems I was wrong. And where are you off to now?'

'To visit the dead,' Steve told her solemnly.

'Across the river? You make it sound so macabre!' She giggled, a sign that she was not quite at ease. 'If you'll hang on a moment, darling, I'll come with you. It won't take me a moment to dress.' She was rattled, she usually refrained from using endearments in Noelle's presence.

'I'm afraid we can't wait,' Steve drawled. 'And this is an expedition strictly for two . . . a honeymoon trip.'

Marcia's face fell. She looked suddenly old, and stared at Steve as if she couldn't believe her ears, while Noelle's apathy was pierced by a dart of triumph. Steve had actually snubbed Marcia!

'A bit belated,' Marcia said nastily.

'It's never too late to mend,' Steve observed airily.

Marcia rallied; she forced an inviting smile.

'The *Serapis* doesn't leave until tomorrow evening. Will you take me to Karnak in the morning? I'm sure Noelle will be too exhausted after a day among the tombs to want to come.'

'Possibly. I'll see you about it after dinner.'

Marcia let them go with a satisfied smile.

'I thought we were leaving tonight?' Noelle asked uncertainly.

'Exactly. We are.'

So he was not going to tell Marcia they were going. She felt a fleeting pity for her. Steve was not kind to his women.

He went on: 'She's becoming tedious and she's got no tact. I can't abide possessive women. Her friends are going on to Aswan with her. We were only incidental until they arrived.'

Oh, sublime understatement! Noelle was still convinced that Marcia's presence on the boat had been prearranged when she discovered Steve was in Cairo, and throughout her aim had been to detach him from his new wife, but she had ceased to amuse him and she was to be discarded without being told of his departure.

'You're cruel sometimes,' she declared as they walked along the landing stage.

'Only sometimes?' he queried mockingly. 'I thought you believed it was my natural bent.'

Noelle made no comment. He had treated her cruelly last night, considering it was well-deserved chastisement.

'Do you always punish severely when you discover a misdemeanour?' she asked with seeming artlessness.

He gave her a crooked smile.

'Always. It's the best way to ensure that the crime is not repeated.'

'Even though as a result the offender may detest and resent you?'

'If so, that's too bad,' he said indifferently.

It was no use, she could not get under his skin. She wished she could detest him, but he had brought down her defences, and she had become vulnerable, she was becoming more and more aware of his sexual magnetism. What did the Greek playwright say? 'One night in a man's arms will make a woman tame.'

Another thought occurred to her. She had married because she wanted children; it had been the strongest of her reasons. Though the first time rarely had that result, it was possible her wish was already granted. Did Steve want them too? Her father thought that was his main reason for surrendering his bachelorhood. Most men wanted a son, and Steve would want to give his all the privileges he had been denied himself—a competent nanny, a public school, Harrow or Eton. Would she be allowed any part in his upbringing? A child was more likely to be a cause of friction than a bond between them, but perhaps she would have a daughter.

'You're very thoughtful, my love,' Steve broke into her cogitations, as they reached the ferry.

'Yes, I've a lot to consider.'

For once he had not caught her thought.

'I hope your conclusions will be satisfactory.'

'So do I,' she agreed.

Noelle's impression of the necropolis was dust, heat and a uniform dun-coloured landscape. The barren Theban Hills were brown, the stone of the monuments weathered to shades of brown and ochre, and since the Nile was shrinking and it was between seasons for cultivations, what vegetation there was appeared brown and withered. Above them a brazen sun shone in a deep blue sky.

The Royal Mortuary Temples are roughly in a line parallel with the river, but divided from it by the flood plain with behind them the gaunt cliffs of the mountains, at a distance of about three miles from the Nile. The valleys in the mountains are honeycombed with tombs and tomb chapels for a distance of some two miles. There are about sixty tombs in the Valley of the Kings, and another seventy in that of the Queens, most notable of the latter being that of Nefertari, the favourite queen of Rameses the Great. She had died young and he appeared to have loved her very much.

It was impossible to visit all the tombs and chapels in this vast area, though their guide conscientiously tried to show them all the high spots. Perhaps the Temple of Queen Hatshepsut impressed Noelle most at Deir-el-Bahri, for it is still in a good state of pre-servation and is built in the form of colonnaded ascending terraces, connected by ramps. The tomb of this great queen is the largest in the Valley of the Kings, for Hatshepsut reigned in Egypt in the place of her young son, calling herself king, and is often depicted as a man. The god's wife, Noelle learned, was the title bestowed on the queen's consort, and Steve told her drily that since the Pharaohs allowed themselves to be worshipped as divine, they had to marry their sisters, for no one of lesser blood could be considered their equal.

The huge, battered Colossi of Memnon excited Noelle's wonder. They had guarded the entrance to Amenhotep the Third's enormous mortuary temple, of which nothing else was left except a few stones and a giant stele.

Visiting the tombs themselves was a failure. The descending passages interspersed by deep shafts to baffle robbers, and pillared vestibules, ending in the burial chamber, gave her claustrophobia. She had always hated being underground.

The wall paintings reminded her of those in Suleiman's house, which had been faithful copies. That was an episode she wanted to forget. After one visit she refused to enter another.

'I'm afraid you're not enjoying it after all,' Steve remarked as they went into the Ramesseum, the Temple of Rameses the Second, called the Great, through the wide outer pylon or gateway, decorated with scenes of the king's wars. Though much was in ruins, there was enough left to give some idea of its ancient grandeur.

'Oh, I am,' she declared gallantly, in spite of her aching feet, for he had thought to please her by coming. 'It's all a bit overwhelming.' She stared at the remains of what had been an enormous statue of the hero king, which their guide said had weighed a thousand tons, the huge head of which reposed on the floor. 'Not exactly modest, were they?'

'It's a little sad,' Steve said thoughtfully. 'All this effort and expense to create lasting monuments to their greatness which would have been buried under the desert sands if it weren't for the zeal of the archaeologists, while their poor mummified bodies moulder in their cases in various museums.'

Noelle recalled that he had expressed a similar trend of thought when they had viewed the Pyramids, and something of the camaraderie of that day seemed to have returned to them.

'But the monuments have lasted,' she pointed out, 'and give a great deal of pleasure and interest to visitors.'

'Who don't care a damn that Rameses defeated the Hittites, and who brings them offerings now?'

In spite of the heat, Noelle shivered, for all said and done, this was a burial ground, and she felt they were desecrating it.

'Centuries hence, tourists may travel to Highgate Cemetery and consider it a showpiece.'

'If it hasn't been blown to bits by a nuclear war. I've willed that I'm to be cremated and my ashes scattered. It's cleaner, and takes up less room.'

Again Noelle shivered; she could not bear to think of all Steve's splendid manhood extinguished.

'You're getting morbid,' she said, 'but if I pre-decease you, I'll hope you'll give me a tomb, like he . . .' she nodded towards the head, 'did for Nefertari.'

For that had been an expression of the great king's love and grief.

'Not me,' he returned, grinning. 'All you'll get is your ashes in an urn.'

'Don't be gruesome!' But he did not love her, he would soon forget her, she thought, and was surprised how much the reflection pained her.

'I think I've seen enough,' she went on, gazing round at the crumbling pillars. 'Sightseeing is tiring and I had a disturbed night.'

She glanced at him sideways, hoping he would show guilt, but his face did not change, and he said casually:

'Did you? When I looked in you were sleeping soundly.'

'You mean . . . you came in again?'

'Naturally I wanted to be sure you were all right.'

'Really? How unexpected, after what you did to me!'

Steve gave her a long, level look and she felt herself flush.

'Though you mayn't believe it, I'm not inhuman,' he told her quietly.

They returned to the boat with Noelle's mind a jumble of temples, carvings and wall paintings. As they were too late for lunch, Steve made a steward rustle up a scratch meal for them. He was silent and preoccupied and she supposed his thoughts had reverted to his business problems. She went to her cabin intending to pack, but was overcome by weariness. She had tried to see too much in too short a space of time. She lay down on the bed, and was soon fast asleep.

Soon she began to dream. She was Nefertari, stretched on her bier, but in possession of all her senses, though she could not move. All around her was the panoply of death—the stone sarcophagus,

the gilded mummy case, and a miscellany of precious
objects to be put into her tomb. With a feeling of
terror she saw a tall man in a white robe holding in
his hands long strips of mummy wrappings. She
wanted to cry out that she was not dead, she could
see and hear, but she could not stir. Then the
Pharaoh appeared, a glittering figure crowned and
carrying his sceptres, with a shining pectoral about
his neck. The attendants—she saw there were a
number of them—prostrated themselves, and
beckoning to one of them, he handed him his
crown, and the flail and crook, the sceptres the
Pharaoh always bears. Then he knelt beside the bier.
To her astonishment, Noelle saw there were tears in
his eyes, and they were grey. He took her in his arms
and rained kisses on her face, and with all her
strength she tried to respond, to show him she was
still alive, but the horror of nightmare shackled her
limbs. She still could not move or speak.

Then the man stood up and said in a harsh voice:
'I don't want an icicle in my bed. Bury her in
Highgate Cemetery.'

She was filled with desperate longing to go to him,
to make some sign, for the Pharaoh's face was
Steve's. She saw him gradually fading away with a
sense of bereavement too terrible to bear, and awoke
with a cry, tears streaming down her face.

'What's the matter?'

She stared at the connecting door which was wide
open and Steve was standing on its threshold.

'Oh, Steve, I dreamed . . .'

He came to her, pushing aside her legs so that he
could sit beside her. He took both her hands in one

of his, and drawing a handkerchief from his pocket, wiped the tears from her face. His eyes, she saw with astonishment, were soft and full of concern.

'A bad dream?'

'Horrible.'

'H'm, the result of wandering round sepulchres in the heat, but you're awake now, my love.' He began to stroke her arms with a soothing motion. 'Tell me your dream.'

'I seemed to be dead, only I wasn't. I was lying on something like this bed. They . . . they were preparing to bury me.' She stopped and shuddered, the miasma of her dream still clinging to her. Steve gently pushed back the hair from her forehead.

'Was I in this dream of yours?'

'Oh yes, you were Pharaoh, in full regalia. You looked . . . magnificent.' She laughed shakily.

'But surely I wasn't assisting in these unpleasant rites?'

'No. You came in and everyone flopped on the floor. Then you stood over me . . . like you did last night.'

He became very still, and his hands slowly clenched on his knees.

'Like last night . . . go on.'

'I wanted to get up, to beg you . . . but I couldn't.' Her despair in the dream came back to her and she cried in anguish. 'But I couldn't move, that was what was so terrible, I was helpless. I wanted to . . . escape, but I couldn't move.'

She covered her face with her hands and shuddered. She had meant she wanted to flee from those horrible men who were preparing her burial, to beseech Steve-Pharaoh to take her away. That he might put a different interpretation upon her words never occurred to her.

'I understand.'

He stood up and his face was like the man in her dream when he had said: 'I don't want an icicle in my bed.'

He looked down at her; she was lying in the same position as she had lain last night when he had come to punish her, and her eyes held the same desperate appeal as when she had besought him to listen to her and he had told her to shut up. A spasm crossed his face, and he spoke harshly:

'For heaven's sake, get up, girl!'

She wilted, and he went on in a softer voice:

'You were overdone with the heat and you're so sensitive, those mausoleums stimulated your imagination too strongly. But you're awake now, and you'd better get on with your packing, or shall I send for a stewardess to do it for you?'

'Oh no, I'll do it.' She swung her legs over the edge of the bed. Steve had again become remote and aloof. Yet he had tried to comfort her. She knew that he despised softness and thought he must be regretting what he would consider a lapse into weakness. She went on:

'I'd like to say goodbye to the Bates. I think they were going to Karnak, but they'll be back by now.'

'I expect so.' He sounded completely disinterested, but he was lingering in her cabin as if he were loath to leave her.

'It isn't a secret, is it? I mean, our departure? You didn't tell Marcia.'

'No, it's not secret, and I suppose I'd better go and tell her now. You thought I was being inconsiderate, didn't you?'

She had thought he was worse than that, and though she disliked and distrusted Marcia she didn't like to think Steve would deliberately hurt her.

'We were in a hurry and I thought she'd make a scene,' he explained.

'Will she make one now?'

He made a grimace. 'Probably, but I'll cope with her.'

Noelle stood up. 'Steve . . .'

'Yes?'

'You won't . . . I mean, if she suggests it . . . take her back with us?'

He looked astonished. 'Why ever should I do that? I've told you before, she's going with these friends of hers to Aswan.' His eyes narrowed. 'You didn't believe they existed, did you?'

She hung her head.

'Remember before you pass judgment again how wrong you were.'

With that he went out on deck.

Noelle sat down again holding her head between her hands, while she went over what had passed in review. Her dream was quite understandable, it was a hotch-potch of her impressions during the day, but Steve's reaction to her distress had surprised her. He had seemed so understanding until she had told him the culmination. Then something had stung him and he had changed completely, she couldn't imagine why, but her own feelings had clarified. In spite of his assault upon her, the rose had revived, she did love him, and his unpredictability was part of his charm. Hugh she had understood thoroughly, she had known what he would do and say in any given circumstances as if he were part of herself, but Steve had all the fascination of an enigma.

With a sigh, Noelle abandoned her unproductive thoughts, washed her face, changed her dress and went in search of the Bates.

She found Mrs Bates lying upon her bed flushed and feverish, and her husband a very worried man.

'She's got a rash,' he told Noelle. 'We didn't go to Karnak as she was feeling poorly, and she's become steadily worse. It may be something she's eaten. I don't think there's a doctor on board.'

'No, but there'll be one in the town.'

She guessed the Colonel was not only fretting over Mary's health, but if her illness was serious, hospitalisation would be very expensive. She laid a cool hand on Mary's forehead, and asked if he had taken her temperature. He admitted he had not, he had no thermometer, but Noelle had. She would go and get it and enquire about a doctor at the office.

'Bless you,' the Colonel said with a faint smile.

Noelle sped up the companionway to the next deck. She would fetch the thermometer first. On the promenade above she encountered Steve.

'Hello? Something wrong?' He put out an arm to check her.

'It's Mary Bates, she's ill.' Breathlessly she told him about Mary's condition and what she proposed to do.

'You won't go near her again,' Steve said forcefully.

'But Steve, I must . . .'

'You will not. You little fool, it may be something infectious and you've already exposed yourself to it.'

'It's probably nothing serious, and I had all the jabs before I came . . .'

'So of course did she.' He held her arm firmly, preventing her from moving. 'Listen to me. You'll go and finish your packing and I'll get a conveyance to take us straight to the airport. We may be able to pick up an earlier flight to Cairo or Alex, there are often cancelled seats, but we must get away at once.'

'But why?' she asked blankly.

'As you say, it may be only a minor ailment, but if the doctor diagnoses something serious we may all be put in quarantine. I must get back, and quickly. Don't tell anyone you've been to see her, understand? You can have a check-up when we get to London.'

She stared at him incredulously.

'Do you never think of anyone but yourself? I won't go, she's my friend, she needs me.'

'She won't, she'll have professional attention.'

'That's another thing. They aren't well off. I think the Colonel's worried about expense.'

'Presumably he's insured. What do you expect me to do? Give him a blank cheque?'

'You wouldn't miss it.'

'Maybe not, but I didn't get where I am by listening to hard luck stories. Besides, he's a gentleman, he wouldn't take it.'

'You don't know. The offer of a loan might relieve him.' Noelle tried to free her arm. 'Let me go, I must get that thermometer.'

'You will do no such thing, I told you you were

not to go near her again and I expect you to obey me.'

Noelle's lips set mutinously, and her eyes were stormy.

'I'm sure the risk is very slight, I don't care about it.'

'But I do.' Steve held her arm in an iron grip and his face was stern. 'Are you going to do what you're told?' She shook her head. 'Very well, then you must be made to.'

He picked her up as if she had been a naughty child and ran up the next flight of stairs as if he found her weight no burden at all. Too confounded to struggle, which would have been undignified as well as useless, since Steve could easily master her, she choked with indignation and outrage.

He dumped her down upon the bed in her cabin, and striving to master her rage, she tried to speak reasonably.

'Steve, you can't really mean we're going to run away without doing anything to help those poor people? I promised . . .'

'You can't be blamed for not keeping it in the face of superior force,' he smiled satirically. 'The old fool should never have allowed you to see his wife when he didn't know what was wrong with her, but they aren't your responsibility and you are mine.' He paused, then added deliberately, 'You're rather precious to me.'

Noelle had always known he would be ruthless where his business interests were concerned, but to try to cloak his inhumanity under a pretence of anxiety for her well-being she could not accept.

'You don't care a damn about me,' she stormed, 'so don't hand me out any soft soap! Go if you must, but let me stay on board. I'll go on to Aswan with them and find my own way back.'

'That's quite out of the question.' He caught hold of her hair, holding a strand on either side of her face and forcing her to look up at him. 'Do you want to stay to nurse Mrs Bates, or to make another assignment with ben Ahmed?'

'Oh God, no!' She tried to free her hair, he was pulling it quite mercilessly. 'How dare you suggest such a thing? Only your corrupt mind would think of it. Oh!' as he gave her hair a tug. 'You're a brute and a bully,' she exploded, 'a cruel beast!'

Steve released her so suddenly she fell back on the bed.

'Couldn't you think of something more original to call me?' he asked sarcastically. 'You're becoming monotonous, and you've never left me in any doubt about your opinion of me. But we're wasting time. You still haven't packed.'

She clenched her hands. 'I'm not coming.'

'Of course you're coming. Are you going to be sensible, or must I lock you in while I make my arrangements?'

She hesitated, but she knew she was defeated. If she continued to defy him he would imprison her until he was ready to drag her ignominiously off the boat.

'And I mean stay in here,' he went on. 'No slipping off to the Bates or trying to contact a doctor.'

Noelle looked at him with wide, accusing eyes. 'I'll stay here since I must, but I think you're utterly selfish, a bully, and in every way despicable.'

'Too bad.' He gave her a derisive grin, and went out.

Noelle restrained the tears of frustration that had risen to her eyes. Tears wouldn't help anyone. Steve had seemed so different when he had comforted her after her nightmare, but now she had the sensation of having been butting her head against a granite wall. He wasn't human, she decided fiercely, he was a computer programmed to produce statistics, incapable of normal feelings. She thought of writing a note to the Colonel, but what could she say? 'My husband forbade me to help you'? No, she couldn't say that, but any expression of regret would sound insincere, and she was too wretched to think up excuses. Mechanically she packed her cases, tidied her hair and powdered her nose. She was already dressed for travelling. She caught sight of the linen hat, which she had overlooked, and on a sudden impulse picked it up and went on deck to throw it overboard. There, she thought, goes the last of my Egyptian . . . honeymoon . . . Honeymoon, what irony! She smiled wryly and went back inside to await her husband's coming, outwardly compliant, inwardly seething with resentment.

CHAPTER EIGHT

FOREST LODGE was situated above the river below the Cliveden woods. It was a solid Georgian house standing in an acre of grounds, surrounded on three sides by trees; on the fourth smooth lawns sloped down to the water, where there was a boathouse and a landing stage. To one side of the house the ground had been levelled to make a tennis court, on the other there were greenhouses where fruit and hot-house flowers were cultivated; there were two full-time gardeners who also acted as chauffeurs when required. Noelle was familiar with the place since she had spent many weekends there with her family prior to her marriage, but now she was coming to it as its mistress, and she had wondered anxiously if she was going to be able to cope with such a large establishment. It was very different from the semi-detached villa where she had lived with her family.

It was late in October and the woods were displaying their autumn glory of russet and gold; though not really cold, the atmosphere seemed chilly after the Egyptian sun.

They arrived in the grey dawn after travelling all night, having hired a taxi at the airport. As Steve had been unable to advise his staff of their sudden return, they were not expected. The house was run by a very efficient housekeeper, a Mrs Ingram, whose duties Noelle had no intention of interfering with, and she hoped the good lady would not resent her. She had, on her previous visits, seemed to be an amiable sort of person, totally unlike the Mrs Danvers of fiction, with her fierce hostility to the new bride, but then Steve had not had a former wife with whom she could be compared.

The house was dark and shuttered when Steve sent the front door bell pealing through the hall. He had a latch key, but the door was bolted as well as locked at night. While they waited, with their luggage piled on the doorstep, Noelle looked at the strip of silver that was the river gliding by below them, for colour had not yet returned to the earth, and tried to realise it was less than twelve hours since she had stood by a different river. She seemed to have been travelling for ever.

Mrs Ingram drew back the bolts and revealed herself in a flannel dressing gown and curlers. She had known at once who had rung that imperious peal and she was quite used to her master arriving at all hours.

'Eh, I'm sorry, sir,' she said, struggling with a yawn. 'We didn't expect you . . .'

'I had a sudden call from the office,' Steve explained. 'I couldn't let you know, but you always keep the bedrooms aired.' He was bundling in their cases. 'Take Mrs Prescott up to the master bedroom, and make her comfortable, she needs to sleep. That's her smaller case, if you can manage that.'

'Yes, sir.' Mrs Ingram picked it up. 'Will you be coming up too, sir?'

'Oh, I'll have a nap in the blue guest bedroom. Tell Jones to bring the car round at eight-thirty. I must be in Town before ten.'

'Yes, sir.' Mrs Ingram smiled at Noelle. 'You know the way, madam?'

She was a stout, elderly person, usually garbed in black and dignity. Her déshabille made her seem homely, even motherly. She followed Noelle up the wide staircase, saying:

'You look all in, madam, but I know the master. If business calls he'll not wait for nobody. I suppose there was some crisis in the City?'

Noelle murmured an affirmative, hardly able to keep her eyes open.

'That man's made of steel,' the good lady ran on. 'Travel all night, work all day, and like as not out somewhere this evening, but you, madam, you look frail, he's fair worn you out.'

Noelle knew her looks belied her, she had a wiry strength that had been necessary for her exacting work, but Steve had taxed it sorely, not so much the actual journey but the emotional scene that had preceded it.

She followed Mrs Ingram into the big room overlooking the river, with its deep-piled white carpet, light oak furniture and Regency striped curtains. The housekeeper turned on the electric stove, suggested a bath and went to run it for her in the adjacent bathroom, extracting what was needed from her case. It was very pleasant to be waited upon, Noelle thought dreamily, and Steve would not be coming to disturb her. Refusing an offer of refreshment, she sank down on the big double bed and was almost immediately asleep.

Mrs Ingram drew the curtains against the brightening day, then glanced almost pityingly at the fair head on the pillows. She had been pleased when her master had decided to get married, it was time he settled down, and the large nurseries at the back of the house were crying out to be filled, the place was built for a family, but she was doubtful about his choice. Noelle looked too delicate to be a good breeder, too fragile to keep pace with her master's imperious demands. He never spared himself and he would expect his wife to live at the same rate as he did. She went out shaking her head to seek Jones the chauffeur-cum-gardener.

Noelle awoke late in the afternoon, and for a moment could not recollect where she was, her gaze wandering around the unfamiliar room, then recollection returned. She was in her new home and lying on the bed she would share with Steve. A quiver of excitement ran along her nerves; at last she was about to begin her married life.

She saw a maid had been in and unpacked for her while she slept, but there were none of Steve's possessions in the room. They must be still in the blue guest room. She got up and dressed in a tweed skirt and sweater; it seemed strange to be wearing warm clothes when in Egypt it would still be broiling. She would ring her mother, she decided, and tell her she was back. She wondered if there were any way by which she could discover how Mary Bates was faring, and whether she was still on the *Serapis*, but she felt unequal to dealing with telecommunications. She had no idea whom she should try to contact. Steve would know, but she was very reluctant to open the subject of the Bates with him, after his display of callousness.

Mrs Ingram met her as she descended the polished wood staircase.

'I hope you feel rested, madam. You would like tea served in the drawing-room?'

'Yes, thank you.'

'The master rang up. He'll be unable to get back tonight.'

Another reprieve—or was it? Hating him, yet she longed for his presence. It was lonely without anyone to talk to, for she dared not be too familiar with the housekeeper.

'Mr Prescott's things haven't been moved from the blue room,' she remarked.

'He gave me no instructions about that, madam. Do you wish me to have them brought into yours?'

Noelle shook her head. 'Better wait for him to tell you.'

'As you say, madam.'

Steve would not be back tonight, but what about tomorrow? Did he intend to go on occupying another room, the one furthest from hers, incidentally? She thought disconsolately of that huge master bedroom, the vast bed; she would feel lost alone in it, a forsaken lamb on an empty mountainside . . . well, it was better than being a sacrificial lamb, wasn't it, exposed to Steve's capricious desires, but she no longer found that prospect daunting.

She went into the gracious drawing-room—sitting-room or living-room were much too commonplace descriptions for it. It was as elegantly furnished as many she had seen in stately homes, in white and gilt. The house was centrally heated, but in addition an electric fire burned in the grate below the marble mantelshelf. Noelle sat down on the velvet-covered couch, and a maid wheeled in an afternoon tea trolley, with a single cup and saucer. I'm a grass widow already, she thought wryly, and wondered how she was going to fill her days. What did ladies of leisure do, needlework, shopping, paying calls? One thing stuck out a mile: she was not going to see much of her husband, and she did not know if she were glad or sorry.

Next day her mother came to lunch at her invitation. Her father was at work, Simon at college, but they would all be delighted to come for a weekend soon, Marjorie suggested hopefully. Noelle said she would be delighted, but she didn't know what Steve's plans were. She would have to ask him if he were agreeable.

Her mother said huffily that she thought the mistress of the house should be able to ask whom she pleased, and Noelle admitted that she had not got round to thinking about entertaining yet. Nor had she brought the family any souvenirs from Egypt; Steve had been recalled so suddenly she had not had time.

'Too bad,' Mrs Esmond said indifferently, and plunged into a flood of chatter about her own concerns. They had never been very close and Noelle would not have dreamed of confiding in her any of the things that really mattered to her. She said goodbye to her almost with relief. At least she had not said how much better she had done for herself than if she had married Hugh, but she knew the thought had been in her mind.

There was a stereogram and a television, which would provide entertainment for the evenings. After her mother had gone, Noelle went for a short walk, and when she came in Mrs Ingram said to her:

'You should get a dog, madam. A dog can be famous company.'

Noelle was pleased with the idea, it would be a companion on her walks. She had never had a dog of her own, though the family had had one when she was a schoolgirl. She remembered being broken-hearted when it died of old age.

Steve came back the following evening. Apprised

of his coming, Noelle had changed into a black dinner gown and was waiting for him in the drawing-room. She had heard his car arrive and had checked an urge to run to meet him; there was still constraint between them over the Bates incident. He had changed into a dinner jacket when he came to join her, and looked tired, but his face lighted up when he saw her. She had been looking at the objects in the various glass-fronted cabinets, and had found the bronze monkey. She had taken it out and was examining it when Steve came in, trying to disguise the rapid beating of her heart. She made a charming picture standing under one of the wall lights, which turned her bare arms to alabaster, and her hair to a mingling of frost and fire, swathed round her well-shaped head.

He came towards her impetuously and she thought he was going to kiss her, but he halted a few paces from her and his face went blank.

'The ice maiden,' he said sotto voce, with a twist of his thin mouth. 'Well, my dear, getting settled in?'

'Yes, thank you,' she returned primly.

His eyes fell on the monkey. 'What have you got there?'

'A piece out of the cabinet. It's rather . . . quaint.'

'Not bad,' he observed indifferently. 'I'd forgotten it was there.'

The bronze he had waited seven years to acquire!

Noelle put it back into the cabinet. She too had caught his fancy, and fired with the desire for possession he had been determined to win her. Now he had done so, he had installed her in his fine house and was content to leave her, forgotten while he followed his own hectic pursuits.

The parlourmaid came to tell them dinner was served. The indoor staff was all female except for the French chef, André, and consisted mainly of foreign girls whom Mrs Ingram sought to train in the way they should go. Ilse had a crush on Steve, but he never noticed she was there. She was from Germany.

Over dinner, served at one end of the big mahogany table, Noelle told him she wanted a dog, and asked if he had any objections.

'None at all—it's a good idea. There are several breeders of pedigree animals in the district.'

'I don't want a pedigree one, I want one that nobody else wants.'

He raised his brows. 'A stray?'

'Yes, one that wouldn't otherwise get a good home.'

She thought he would protest that he didn't want a low-bred cur profaning his beautiful home, but he said gently:

'You have a generous nature. We'll go to a dogs' home.'

She had not expected him to accompany her, and she asked when he would be free, he seemed to be so busy.

'I am, but I can spare an hour on Sunday morning.' It was then Friday. 'Tomorrow I'll be away all day, there's a new factory site in the Midlands I want to inspect.'

'On a Saturday? Don't you have a holiday?'

He gave her a crooked smile.

'I've just had a holiday, and with a vast network to oversee, I don't take days off.'

'You're heading for a coronary,' she warned.

'How can I when I've no heart?'

A quibble which indicated that some of her shafts had gone home. Noelle felt a momentary compunction, then she remembered Mary Bates lying feverish in her cabin and Steve's callous attitude towards the invalid and her own distress. He *had* no heart.

'Your things are still in the blue room, I believe,' she said abruptly, changing the subject, 'unless you've had them moved.'

Steve's eyes met hers with a quizzical expression.

'I'm staying there for the present. You still look tired, my love, and you found my ... er .... attentions rather exhausting.'

She blushed, and he laughed derisively.

'Painful memories, eh? Don't worry, my love, they won't be repeated.'

She felt chilled. Did he mean they were to live together as strangers? She in her glass case, he absorbed in his business ventures? Such a prospect seemed unutterably bleak. She stared at her plate, wondering what exactly she did want. A little voice at the back of her brain murmured, 'To be loved.' But that was ridiculous; Steve could not love anyone.

He went on coolly:

'I would like you, however, to assume your social duties. I want to give a dinner party next month, to introduce you to the neighbourhood, and to invite some of my new executives. My secretary is making out a list of names and addresses for you so that you

can send out the invitations. I would prefer the en-
velopes to be hand-written, and of course you must
insert the names on the cards in your own fair hand.
As for the catering, you must consult André and Mrs
Ingram. They've organised such functions before.'

He was aloof, withdrawn, quite impersonal.

Noelle said meekly that she would do her best to
carry out his wishes, for this was one of his reasons
for taking a wife. She would do her best to carry out
this duty to make up for having failed in others.

'That's a good girl,' he said absently.

In the drawing-room, while she poured coffee into
the exquisite Dresden cups, he exclaimed:

'Oh, by the way, I've brought you a present.'

He went out into the hall and returned carrying a
large cardboard box, which he placed beside her.

'Open it and see if it fits.'

It was a mink coat. Though Noelle would not as a
rule wear real fur, she could make an exception of
mink, for the animals were not trapped, but raised
on farms, and the coat was beautiful. Steve held it
for her so that she could slip her arms into it. It
might have been made for her.

'I've had enough experience in women's gear to
be able to gauge your measurements accurately,'
Steve said with satisfaction, and she wondered if he
had ever given Marcia mink. 'Our guests will all
have fur coats, and in that you'll look as fine as any
of them.'

His words marred her pleasure in his gift. He had
bought it not so much to please her, but to impress
his acquaintances. She slipped it from her shoulders,
folding it reverently, for her shop training had taught

her to respect expensive clothes, and she knew from the quality of the fur that this coat had cost a packet.

'Thank you very much,' she said formally. 'It'll be a great comfort when the weather turns really cold.' He had been looking at her eagerly, as if he hoped for a warmer expression of gratitude, and she added quickly: 'You're very kind and very generous,' but the words were uttered mechanically. She was remembering what he had said when she had asked him to help Colonel Bates; he had been neither then.

'Well, at least those adjectives are different from those you usually bestow upon me,' he remarked caustically, and immersed himself in the evening papers. Ilse came to remove the coffee tray, and Noelle asked her to take the coat upstairs. Noelle perused a novel, very conscious of her husband's presence, and wishing he would talk, tell her of his day's doings, but she dare not question him, fearing to expose her ignorance of the commercial world and thus earn his scorn. But he did not speak until he said it was bedtime, wished her goodnight and they went to their separate rooms.

Noelle went into her room, where the bed had been turned down, her nightgown laid out, and the curtains drawn. Mrs Ingram trained her staff well. She need not fear that Steve would come to her, he had made it very clear that he had no such intention, but she derived no comfort from the knowledge, instead she had a feeling of anti-climax, and the bed looked very big and empty.

Steve was absent all Saturday, returning after she

was in bed. It almost seemed as if he were trying to avoid her, but on Sunday, true to his promise, he drove her to the dogs' home. Noelle found it heart-breaking; so many eager affectionate animals longing to bestow their love and loyalty upon some human being, for though they were well treated, and the home was a sanctuary with no fear of destruction hanging over them, they lacked the individual at-tention for which they yearned.

She chose a rather odd-looking creature of mixed ancestry. Rough-haired, he was some sort of terrier, with a whiskery face, slate grey in colour, legs neither long nor short, with one flop ear, the other pricked, but such an intelligent, wistful look in his brown eyes that she could not resist him.

'He was found in a wood, tied to a tree, aban-doned,' the warden told them.

'Oh, how can people be so cruel!'

Noelle imagined the dog's state of mind when he found himself deserted by those he had trusted.

'Better than being turned out on a motorway, as some of them are.'

'Not really?'

'I'm afraid so.'

They were expected to give a small donation, but Steve made out a generous cheque. Going home with the dog on her lap, again thinking of the Bates, Noelle remarked:

'It seems you've more feeling for dogs than people.'

'Dogs are not mercenary, and they're more grate-ful.'

Noelle stared out of the window beside her, wondering if that were intended as a dig at her. She would gladly have exchanged her wealth and comfort, her pearls and mink, for true companionship, and warm human sympathy, such as Hugh would have given her, but Steve only saw her as an adornment to his home and had ceased to want her in his bed.

He was away most of the following week, and Noelle found solace in the company of Pickles, as she called her dog. He took to life at Forest Lodge as an otter to water, accepting two good meals a day, his basket and walks in the woods as if he had never known anything less. He was suspicious of the staff, declaring war on the gardeners, who complained about the holes he dug in the flower-beds, but he gave Noelle wholehearted devotion, slept in her room at night, to Mrs Ingram's disapproval, and followed her everywhere. Fortunately he tolerated Ilse, who was a dog-lover, for Noelle foresaw that there would be times when she would have to leave him.

The following weekend, Steve had to attend a conference, and he suggested she should ask her family to stay to keep her company, which she was glad to do. They arrived on the Friday evening after he had left, her parents and Simon, who had a few days' leave. Mrs Esmond acted as though she and not her daughter were mistress of the house, convinced Noelle had no idea how to run it. She antagonised Mrs Ingram with her prying, and Noelle had to soothe her down, reminding her that her mother would be going on Sunday night, and she could ignore her interference.

Marjorie Esmond criticised Steve's absence—surely Noelle could have accompanied him to the conference? Wives often did.

'Oh, I didn't want to go,' Noelle declared, concealing the fact that it had not been suggested. 'I think men are better on their own at these business do's.'

Her mother snorted. 'That may be the modern point of view, but I don't believe in married couples being separated. I've never slept a night apart from your father since we were married.'

Noelle concealed a smile, thinking her father would not have minded an occasional holiday from his wife's domineering presence, but she said nothing.

Mr. Esmond, more perceptive, was troubled by her appearance. She did not look happy.

'It's working out all right?' he asked anxiously when they were alone.

'Oh yes, Daddy, why shouldn't it?'

'I don't know, but you don't look like a blooming newlywed. Is Steve kind to you?'

'Oh, very, he's too generous, but I'm having to get acclimatised to life at Forest Lodge. Takes a bit of getting used to.' Not for worlds would she want him to suspect that Steve neglected her.

'Well, it's a bit bigger than our semi,' he laughed, but he was not satisfied.

Simon's company was pure joy; with him Noelle recovered some of her normal gaiety, that had been quenched when Hugh died, and not until now revived. On the Sunday morning, her parents having decided to go to church, Marjorie wanting, her daughter suspected, to roll up in the Prescott limousine, she and her brother played truant. Simon lent her a pair of jeans, which she wore with an old sweater, and she unearthed a pair of wellingtons in the greenhouse, where someone had left them. They went down to the boathouse, where Steve housed a punt, and an inflatable dinghy. They blew up the latter with a foot pump, found to their joy it was watertight and paddled out into mid-stream.

It was a fine, windy day, the breeze stripping the last leaves from the trees and driving white clouds across the sky—an unusual day for November, which is usually misty and overcast. Pickles was supremely happy, chasing water voles and scattering ducks, one ear down, one ear up, as he splashed through the reeds. The difficulties and traumas that had accumulated since her marriage were blown away by that same healing breeze. With her tangled hair flowing down her back, a lovely colour in her cheeks, Noelle laughed and chaffed with Simon, as she sat in the dinghy, wielding her paddle with more splashing than progress, and the boat rocked and danced on the rippling water as if it too were imbued with their effervescent spirits. Noelle looked about sixteen, to Simon's seventeen, she who had almost forgotten what it was like to be young and irresponsible.

A racing craft went by, taking advantage of the fine day to put in some practice, eight oars in perfect rhythm, their diminutive cox crouched in the stern. They ceased their foolery to allow it passage undisturbed.

'Do you row at college?' Noelle asked.

Simon made a face. 'No, too much hard work, those poor devils work at it like galley slaves. Messing about on the river is fun, but you have to have a vocation to want to race. Does Steve row?'

'I suppose so.' She was vague about her husband's recreations. He had occasionally taken her out in the punt before they were engaged, and she recalled his lithe graceful figure in flannels, as he had manoeuvred the pole. He played a hard game of tennis, but not with her, she was not in his class. He had not had much leisure for sport in his hard-working youth, but whatever he did, he did well.

'Shame about that conference, I'd like to have seen him again.'

'Oh, you will eventually.' Noelle looked at her muddy boots and stained jeans. She would not have dared to dress like this if there had been any chance of Steve returning, and seeing her so clad. Always he expected her to appear well groomed and immaculate as became an ex-model, nor did she think he would sympathise with the fun they were enjoying in the dinghy. It was unbecoming to the chatelaine of his home.

Simon saw her face had clouded and grinned impishly.

'Poor old Sis, does your new position take some living up to?'

She said with dignity: 'It's no sinecure being mistress of Forest Lodge.'

'But it was for that you married him, didn't you?'

'I did not!'

She looked affectionately at her brother's tousled hair, so like her own, his mischievous blue eyes. Did he realise he owed his college fees to Steve's generosity? But if he did it would not trouble him, for he had a happy philosophy that those who had should share with those who had not. He called it socialism. But he might have been upset to learn that Steve's assistance was part of her bride price.

'Was it for love, then?' Simon looked disbelieving. 'Of course he's a wonderful guy, but you never looked at him as you used to look at Hugh.'

'Fancy you noticing that,' she mocked. She hadn't loved Steve then, but she did now, and Hugh had receded into the limbo of the past. 'There are different kinds of loving,' she said thoughtfully, trailing one hand in the water.

'Are there? I've always found my girl-friends all too boringly similar,' Simon told her with an air of manly wisdom that made her want to laugh. He looked at his watch, which fortunately was water-proof. 'I say, isn't it nearly lunch time? I'm hungry and the church parade will have returned.'

'Yes, we must go back.'

Noelle reluctantly picked up her paddle and with a vigorous stroke sent the dinghy heading for the bank. The carefree interlude was over, she must make herself look respectable for the formal meal served with all the trimmings in the big dining-room, the room where the dark panelling made an effective frame for her hair. Her mother delighted in being served in state, but Noelle herself would have preferred a picnic snack on the river bank. But to be fair, it was a treat for Marjorie to eat a meal she had not had to cook herself.

Simon deflated the dinghy, and a filthy, panting, but very happy little dog joined them in answer to Noelle's call. They themselves were no less dirty and bedraggled. Most of the accumulated dust in the boathouse seemed to have been wiped off on Simon's jeans, and Noelle had caught her sleeve on a nail, the tear and fast unravelling wool adding to her unkempt appearance. They started up the long mown slope towards the house, both laughing joyously at some nonsense of Simon's.

Then Noelle stopped dead as if she were shot, all her animation dying away as she exclaimed:

'Oh, my God!'

For at the top of the slope Steve was standing, watching their approach, with a scowl on his handsome face.

CHAPTER NINE

STEVE was of course immaculate; never had Noelle seen him in need of a shave. He wore a suede car coat over his well tailored business suit, and his polished shoes reflected the pale sunlight; only his dark hair was ruffled by the breeze. Noelle had become painfully conscious of her own dishevelled looks, feeling sure that was the cause of her husband's scowl. Mrs Steven Prescott should always appear well groomed and chic, as if she had just stepped out of a ... glass case. She had never dreamed he might come back today, believed him to be far away, but mingled with her dismay was the disturbance to her senses which an unexpected sight of him always caused, ever since that night on the *Serapis*, when she had been unwillingly awakened to the needs of her own body as well as his. If only he had been a little later she would have changed for lunch.

Simon and Pickles had no inhibitions about their appearance. Both went racing up the slope to meet him, Simon shouting:

'Shiver my timbers, it's the boss man himself!'

He seized Steve's hand and pumped it vigorously, while Pickles, after marring the perfection of shoes and trousers, by shaking himself vigorously, rolled on his back, waving muddy paws, hoping for attention.

'You seemed pleased to see me,' Steve remarked to Simon, rubbing Pickles' stomach with the toe of one mud-splattered shoe. His toleration of the mongrel always surprised Noelle, and Pickles adored him. His eyes were fixed on the aloof figure of his wife, as he went on: 'Well, you do look a trio of ragamuffins!'

'Who cares, we've been having fun!' Simon cried. Some of his exuberance waned as he added doubtfully: 'We had the dinghy out—you don't mind, sir?'

'Don't call me sir, I'm your brother.'

Simon looked a little startled at this claim to kinship, then grinned broadly. Steve continued: 'I don't mind in the least so long as you both can swim, though I didn't know your sister is partial to dinghies. I've only been in a punt with her.'

Noelle had a vivid recollection of sunny afternoons, herself reclining in the stern of the punt clad in a white pleated skirt—Steve considered trousers unfeminine—a middy blouse and a wide straw hat, while he manipulated the pole; the cool, dignified unflappable Miss Esmond, a very different picture from the scarecrow she must now look in her torn sweater and disgraceful jeans.

'Oh, I can swim like a seal,' Simon assured him. 'Sis isn't exactly Olympic standard, but she can keep afloat.'

How little Steve knew about her, Noelle thought, to be unaware that she could swim, or had he forgotten? She was a better performer than Simon was implying; she and Hugh had often visited the baths together. She had not swum since he died. But Steve always saw her as a glamorous mannequin, and didn't connect her with sport. No glamour about her now, with her windblown hair, no make-up on her face, boots and jeans plastered with river mud.

'I'm sorry you found me like this,' she said apologetically, 'but I didn't expect you home today or I'd have been properly dressed.'

'I've only dropped in to collect some papers,' he explained, studying her with a hooded stare. In her boyish garb, she and Simon might have been twin youths, and of the two, she was the dirtier. 'I'm sorry to have interrupted your . . . fun.'

'Oh, we were coming in to get ready for lunch. Simon and I always enjoy messing about on the river.'

Steven looked as though he considered 'messing' was an appropriate word. There was something odd about his demeanour, as if he had received an unexpected shock, but surely discovering his wife behaving like a hoyden could not have been as devastating as all that? Something must have gone awry at his conference. Simon and Pickles had gone on ahead, and she said anxiously: 'Has anything gone wrong?'

Not that he would tell her if it had. He never discussed his business problems with her, she was completely excluded from that side of his life, which of late seemed to entirely absorb him.

'No, things don't go wrong when I'm in command,' he declared arrogantly, 'at least, not in business.' Then he added in a completely different tone: 'I was glad to see you looking so happy. I'm afraid my coming spoilt it.'

'Of course it didn't. I was pleased to see you, and it was time we came in anyhow.'

Noelle did not realise how her face had changed when she caught sight of him, as if a light had been extinguished. He had seen her in the distance, all laughing gaiety, but the sparkle had vanished, when she beheld him.

'Simon and I have always been pals,' she said vaguely.

'Yes, and he's nearer your age than I am.' He gave a short sigh. 'You always appeared so sophisticated when you were modelling, I hadn't realised before you aren't much more than a kid.'

She smiled nervously, wondering what that remark was in aid of. She had not seemed a kid to him when he had found her with Omar. Kids were punished with a spanking if physical chastisement was considered necessary, but what he had done to her could only be inflicted upon an adult woman.

'I'm twenty-three,' she reminded him, 'don't pretend you didn't know.'

'In years perhaps, but in that rig-out you look more like fourteen.'

So it was not only her appearance that was annoying him but the gap in years between them, but it had never been a sensitive point before. He was probably thinking that Marcia, or his other girl-friends, would never so demean themselves as to spend a Sunday morning splashing about in a rubber dinghy.

'Oh, I'll soon change that,' she said brightly. 'Are you staying to lunch?'

'I'm afraid I can't. I'll just say hello to your parents and then I must be off again.'

It was Noelle's turn to sigh. A wife and a home seemed unnecessary appendages for a man who was always somewhere else. They were slowly wending their way up the bank, and her boot caught in a loose turf; being much too big for her, it was dragged half off, and she paused to pull it on again, standing on one leg to do so. Steve watched her with an inscrutable expression, but did not offer to support her.

'If you're going to make a habit of this sort of thing, you'd better get some boots that fit,' he observed.

'Oh no, I shan't, since you disapprove.'

'But I haven't said . . .'

'It wasn't necessary, you looked.'

'My dear girl, why do you always try to make me out an ogre?' He sounded exasperated.

'I'm sure I don't, but a good wife should try to please her husband.'

'An excellent sentiment.' But he didn't sound as if he appreciated it. They moved on again, and Noelle summoned up courage to ask the question that had been much on her mind and for which no suitable opportunity had presented itself.

'Would it be possible to make enquiries about the Bates? The cruise must have been over long since and I would like to know if they got home safely.'

'If they want to communicate with you, they'll write.'

'But if Mary was very ill they may be stuck somewhere. She might ... have died. Wouldn't the agency know their address?'

'It might not want to divulge it.'

'I'm sure you can find out if you want to. You always can.'

'What a touching faith in my infallibility!' he mocked. 'I could ask Marcia, she'll know what happened.'

Noelle stood still.

'Are you in touch with her?' she demanded.

'Not at the moment, but I'm bound to run across her sooner or later.'

Noelle wished she had not spoken; the last thing she wanted to do was to give Steve an excuse to contact Marcia Manning, if he were not already doing so. He was looking at her with a mischievous expression, well knowing how she felt about the other woman—and hadn't she good cause to resent her? Noelle thought bitterly.

'Oh, forget it,' she said hastily.

They moved on; they were nearly up to the top now. The breeze had strengthened, was becoming a gale. Dead leaves swirled around them, Noelle's hair blew out from her face and across Steve's chest. With an exclamation she jerked her head, as a strand of the fine, silky stuff caught on his coat button.

'Keep still, you'll scalp yourself!'

Nervous as a thoroughbred filly, she tried to edge away, pulling at her hair, but he put his arm about her to still her, pressing her against his side, while with his other hand he sought to disentangle the lock of hair. Since their return he never touched her if he could avoid it, and this was the first time they had been close. Noelle's blood leaped at the contact, in every nerve she was aware of him. Would it be ever thus? she thought wildly, hating him for his ruthless egoism, deploring his callousness, and yet she was drawn to him as by a magnet. He was the rock she needed to lean upon, the protection that she had so sorely missed with Hugh's death, and surely he could not be without feeling when he was so kind to her little dog? She herself was feeling much too much, her limbs were starting to tremble, and she said breathlessly:

'Have you got a knife? Cut it off.'

'Sorry, I don't carry lethal weapons.'

But he had as deadly ones—his masculinity, his sexual attraction. His breath stirred her hair, his arm was a steel band about her, her blood was in a tumult, and her knees threatened to give way. She wanted to cry out; Oh, Steve, Steve, let's start again; forget all the bitter things we've said to each other. I believe I love you, hard and unbending as you are, and you . . . .

He didn't believe in love, he had told her so several times. All she could hope for was a resurgence of desire, that fierce, blasting force that had scared her twice already. Steve felt no tenderness towards her and would only sneer if she confessed to a change of heart. He might even reject her. So she remained dumb, and at last she was free.

'Thank you,' she murmured, sweeping her hair together in one hand. She could not look at him.

'Don't mention it, it was a pleasure, but perhaps we'd better walk farther apart, unless you want a repetition.'

Apart—yes, they were apart all right, Noelle thought sadly. She heard her mother's voice through an open window, carried to her on the wind.

'Steve here? But where have they got to?' and Simon's laughing reply:

'Oh, they're necking on the lawn. You'd think they would have got over that by now.'

Noelle blushed fierily and ran into the house.

Mrs Esmond did her best to make Steve change his mind, insisting he should stay at least for lunch, almost as if it were her house, Noelle thought a little resentfully, but he was adamant. The sun went in, and the sky became overcast as he left, as if he had taken the sunshine with him.

'It seemed almost as if he wanted to get away,' Marjorie declared.

It wasn't the first time Noelle had thought the same thing. Was Steve trying to avoid her?

She spent the afternoon playing records on the stereogram for Simon's amusement, but he only cared for pop music, which made her head ache.

In the evening the Esmonds went back to London and Noelle was left alone with Pickles.

The invitations for the dinner party were issued and the replies trickled in. Noelle and Mrs Ingram compiled a list of the acceptances. Some of the guests were coming from a distance and would stay the night.

All the leaves had fallen from the trees, and the nights were long, the days dreary. Steve said Noelle must have a new dress for the dinner, though she considered she had far too many clothes already.

'White,' he told her. 'I like you best in white.'

'It'll look well against the dark panelling in the dining-room, won't it?' she said acidly.

He seemed puzzled by her tone, having completely forgotten what he had said about her hair, but she knew she was to be the principal decoration at his party. That was why he had married her, wasn't it?

'Now you mention it, so it will,' he agreed.

She then surprised both him and herself by asking if she might buy it at Forbes Fashions. She had not been near the place since Hugh's death, unable to bear the associations it held for her, and had obtained employment elsewhere, but now she felt an urge to see it again.

'Sentimental memories?' Steve asked, curling his lip.

'Not exactly, just a whim.'

'Oh, you women and your whims,' he jeered.

But he did not object, neither did he offer to accompany her. It was not exactly sentiment that was prompting her, but a need to lay a ghost.

Noelle had spent her childhood, as also had Hugh, in an Essex village, to which she often looked back with nostalgia, but when commuting became more and more expensive, both families had moved into suburbia. As soon as she left school, she had gone to work for Forbes. Hugh, two years older, and related to the management, was already established there. His designs were original and he had had a way with women customers. It had not been long before she was promoted to modelling on account of her unusual beauty, and her tall slight figure, though she was below the standard height, but Hugh had insisted there was still time for her to grow, and she inspired him. Some of his most successful creations were modelled on her.

But although it was little more than two years since she had left, Noelle found the establishment completely changed, so fast is the pace of modern life. Redecorated and redesigned, the salon where she had first seen Steve had been enlarged, its layout altered so much she did not recognise it. Most of the staff also was comprised of newcomers, but the head saleswoman—in France she would have been called the *directrice*—was the same, but she was far too professional to remind Noelle of her former status. Mrs Steven Prescott was an important client, not to be confounded with the wisp of a girl who had started by running errands for her. Nor was it tactful to allude to her prior attachment. She only permitted herself one hint, and that was of reproach.

'We're honoured that you've decided to patronise us, madam.'

'I couldn't come before,' Noelle said frankly. 'It was too painful.'

The saleswoman's face momentarily softened; they had all been very fond of Hugh.

'I understand, madam.' Then it hardened. 'But we can't allow sentiment to interfere with business.'

A pronouncement of which Noelle was sure Steve would approve. But though she looked here and there, seeking something that would revive for her the memory of the young boy and girl who had worked, laughed and loved there, the once familiar surroundings were too much changed. Their images had left no lasting impression, it was just a shop.

She chose a heavy ivory silk gown, with a skirt falling in straight classic folds, and a draped bodice, but without sleeves. The saleswoman suggested something more dramatic would be more fitted to her position, make her seem more mature, but Noelle stuck to the ivory silk. If Steve wanted her to appear young and virginal, it would fit the bill that he would be paying. She left it to have a small alteration made, and in due course it was delivered. She tried it on when she went to dress for dinner, and hearing Steve's voice in the passage speaking to one of the maids—he was home early for once—she called to him to come and see if he approved of it.

He hesitated on the threshold, for he had never entered the room since she had been occupying it. His eyes went towards the bed, and then to her white-robed figure. He had changed into a velvet jacket and dress trousers, with a frilled shirt. The costume had the effect of giving him the elegance of a Regency buck, though he himself would have derided such a description. He prided himself upon being a man of the people, though wealth and the society he now mingled with had inevitably polished him. He took something out of his pocket as he came towards her, and his eyes had kindled.

'Exquisite, my love, and here's something to give

the finishing touch.'

He handed her a flat case, and when she opened it, the sparkle of diamonds met her gaze.

'Let me fasten it for you.'

The gems were cold on her neck, but his fingers at her nape set her blood on fire. He stepped back to view the effect.

'Frozen fire,' he said with a crooked smile.

Subtly the description stung her.

'You wanted me to wear white,' she flashed, 'and fire melts ice.'

'Or do you mean diamonds do?' He came nearer, an unmistakable look in his eyes. 'You're a siren, a temptress,' he told her hoarsely, before she could object to his slur. Then she was crushed against the velvet jacket, his lips caressing the white column of her throat, lingering in the hollow behind her ear. Neither had a thought to the damage he might be doing to the freshness of her new dress. Noelle could feel the hard thudding of his heart, just above her own, the pressure of his thighs through the clinging folds of her dress. He was becoming thoroughly aroused, and she felt a surge of triumph. She still had the power to excite him.

His mouth came down on hers, hard and demanding, and her lips parted under its insistence. Tremors were running up and down her spine, and she melted in his arms.

The telephone rang.

All the rooms in the house were connected to a main switchboard in the hall outside the housekeeper's room, and each had its own microphone. Usually there was someone within hearing to answer it. Noelle rarely used it, but someone must have seen Steve go into her room, and the call was probably for him.

Steve swore under his breath, tightening his grip of her, but the phone rang on insistently. Training would not permit him to ignore it. Reluctantly he released her and went to lift the receiver. She heard him say:

'Put the call through to the blue room. I'll speak to her in there.'

Then he was gone. Noelle in her turn swore: 'Damn, oh, damn!' For Steve had been on the verge of taking her, giving her a chance to reverse her former coldness, to express her love. Then two things registered: he had given her diamonds, and had thought she had melted to show not love but gratitude, and the phone call had been from a woman— a woman he had not wanted to speak to in his wife's presence. Slowly she took off her party dress, laying it carefully on the bed, and slipped on a black and gold caftan. She dropped the diamond necklace on her dressing table and looked at it with distaste. She had no passion for gems at all, but Steve believed they could buy all a woman had to give. She gave a long sigh, and went down to dinner.

Over the meal Steve was remote, seeming pre-occupied, though he gave her several long, considering looks. She made no attempt to talk, for her thoughts were following one big question mark. Who was the lady who had torn him from her arms? It might have been his secretary, but it was much more likely to be someone with whom he had made an assignment. She knew it was useless to ask him, he would only give her an evasive answer. If he were having affairs, he was discreet, no whisper of them reached Forest Lodge, but then the wife was always the last to learn of them.

When they had finished, he followed her into the drawing-room, swallowed the cup of coffee she poured for him, then said he was afraid he must go out.

That came as no surprise, it was a confirmation of her suspicions.

'Might one ask where?' she asked with reproach in her eyes.

'I have to go into the city. The board have decided to call an emergency meeting to consult about a threatened strike.'

Had it taken him all dinner time to think up that one? She didn't believe a word of it.

'I shan't see you again tonight,' he went on, 'unless . . .?' He left the word hanging, a question between them, and he looked suddenly eager.

'Oh, I shan't sit up,' she said quickly. 'I'll say goodnight now.'

Yet he lingered, seeming undecided, then he shrugged his shoulders.

'I suppose I've offended you again.'

Thinking of his treachery, for was he not going to meet another woman, Noelle said in a cold voice:

'You have, but you can't help your nature, can you?'

Steve flushed angrily, took a step towards her, where she sat on the sofa, exotically beautiful in the gorgeous caftan, and she, fearing he was about to offer her some violence, instinctively raised her arm to ward him off.

Steve gave a harsh laugh and went out of the room, banging the door behind him.

Pickles, sensing she was hurt, scrambled on to her lap and licked her nose. Careless of her clothes, Noelle gathered him into her arms and dropped a few tears on his rough coat.

They rarely met at breakfast, Steve having his earlier than she did, and she very often had hers brought up to her room when she only required coffee and toast. He was in to dinner the next night, and they treated each other with chill politeness. She asked, hoping to embarrass him, how his meeting had gone, and he returned equably that they thought they could avert the strike. She persisted:

'Wasn't it an odd time to call a conference? Even if it was an emergency?'

'Someone had come up with a possible solution. We were all anxious to hear it as soon as possible.'

No, she could never get any change out of Steve.

The day before the dinner she received a letter in a strange hand by the afternoon post. It was postmarked from a town in Devon, and there was a folded enclosure, which dropped out when she opened the letter, and turned to the signature. It was from Mary Bates. So she was all right and back in the West Country cottage, where she had told her they lived. She settled down to peruse it.

Mary wrote: 'I'm sure you will be glad to know that we got back safely and all is well. It turned out I had a touch of food poisoning, nothing catching, in fact we were able to continue the trip. I'm sorry I've been so long in writing to you, but there was quite an accumulation of correspondence and whatnot to deal with on our return—you know Harry is secretary to the local branch of the British Legion and I'm president of the W.I. Well, my dear, let me at last thank you and your kind husband for all you did for us.' Noelle read the sentence twice. What could she mean? 'I quite understand why Mr Prescott didn't want you to contact me again, though I was sad not to be able to say goodbye to you. He thinks the world of you and naturally didn't want you to run the slightest risk, but we did appreciate his prompt action in finding a doctor for me and for the lovely fruit and flowers he had sent on board. As for the enclosed, please return it to him with our most grateful thanks. It turned out we didn't need it, the insurance covered everything, but it was a great comfort to know we had it when we didn't know what we might be let in for, and it was so very considerate of your dear husband to offer us a loan, for of course we would have repaid it eventually.'

The letter continued with descriptions of the places visited, their journey home, etc., etc.—but Noelle read no more. She picked up the enclosure and unfolding it, saw it was a cheque for a thousand pounds made out to Colonel Bates and the signature was Steven Prescott.

Noelle stared at it in bewilderment. Why, oh, why had he done all that and never told her? He knew she had been anxious about her friends. Was it a perverse pleasure in allowing her to think the worst of him? Pride, that since she could so misjudge him, he would not undeceive her? Or was he ashamed to admit such compassion for a pair of indigent tourists, when he had built up an image of himself as a hard, unsentimental tycoon?

He had asked her more than once not to jump to wrong conclusions, but she accepted outward appearances both with regard to Marcia and to the Bates. She had accused him of being heartless and callous and he had refused to defend himself, closing up like a clam. He must be far more sensitive than she had ever imagined beneath the carapace of scornful indifference in which he had armoured himself as protection on his upward climb to success. With sudden insight, she realised that he needed love perhaps more than a less self-sufficient man, but he had never had it, not even from his mother, and so he declared he despised it. He had told her the women he favoured only wanted what he could give them, and probably believed that if he were stripped of his wealth, no one could care for him. She herself had married him not because she loved him but for what he could do for her family, and he knew it. He didn't expect love from her, but he had hoped to find a warm, responsive mate, but she, poor scared rabbit, had been frightened by his lovemaking and called out for Hugh, who had been not half the man Steve was.

They had loved, yes, but with more affection than passion. If they had married they would have been well suited and quite happy, occupied with their boutique, but they would never have scaled any heights of rapture. What she felt for Steve was quite different. If he had been like Hugh she would not have been scared of him, it was the intensity of his feelings that had dismayed her, but he had lit an answering spark in her, which if it were fanned into flame would produce a fire which would weld them together in mutual ecstasy that could lay the foundation for a deep and lasting love.

But Steve had come to believe he repelled her, and that even a diamond necklace could not overcome her revulsion, so he had put her away like the bronze monkey, to be taken out and admired by envious friends, who had no idea of the barrenness of their union. He was too virile a man to go without a woman for long, and she could not blame him for solacing himself with Marcia and the woman over the telephone.

With a sigh she folded up Mary Bates' letter, and looked at the bold, black signature on the cheque, so characteristic of the writer. She must return it to Steve and make some sort of apology, which would not be easy, for she too was proud and sensitive and dreaded his mockery. She decided she would wait until after the dinner party. If she acquitted herself to Steve's satisfaction he would be in an indulgent mood, he might even . . . no, she must not expect more than a polite acceptance of her regret for her unjustifiable accusations, and she would be lucky if she got that.

CHAPTER TEN

THE night of the party was clear and without fog, presenting no traffic problems. The original invitation list had been enlarged to include some of the more distinguished neighbours, including a Member of Parliament and a Lord and Lady Falconbridge who had an estate in Buckinghamshire. Lord Falconbridge was chairman of one of Steve's companies. Her husband had briefed Noelle beforehand as to the status and characteristics of each guest, but when faced with the whole horde of them, she had difficulty in labelling them. Lady Falconbridge was identifiable at once, a thin domineering woman whose strident voice was audible all over the room. Steve moved among them, distinguished in his evening clothes, and though his subordinates had been chosen for force and drive, he was unmistakably the boss man as Simon had called him. Moreover, he was the best-looking man there, his figure still slim, whereas many of his contemporaries were putting on weight, and Noelle noticed how the eyes of the female guests followed him. All of them were stylish, well-groomed women, even the more matronly ones, but they did not intimidate her. They were types with which she was familiar, having seen many of them literally undresssed in the trying-on cubicles of Forbes Fashions or very similar ones. Several recognised her from her modelling days, and she was amused to notice their slight embarrassment, wondering if they should betray their previous knowledge of her. She soon settled that query for them, being unashamed of her origins.

'We've met before, Mrs So-and-so, at the 19— collection, I believe it was.'

That started a conversation about clothes and all stiffness vanished. She overheard one woman say to her husband:

'She was the loveliest mannequin I've ever seen. I'm not surprised Steve married her.'

Aperitifs consumed, they went in to dinner. Noelle

sat at one end of the polished table, divided from her husband by all its gleaming length; she could not even see him for the floral arrangement in its centre.

The table looked very impressive, with lace place mats, silver cutlery and the array of cut glass wine glasses beside each plate. The dinner, from the stuffed avocados to the rum babas and Stilton cheese, was perfection. André had excelled himself. Ilse and another girl in smart black uniforms with little muslin aprons and caps waited on them, having been carefully rehearsed by Mrs Ingram.

The room was panelled in dark wood from floor to ceiling, and as had been suggested, Noelle's silvergilt hair shone against the sombre background, as also did her ivory dress and snowy neck and shoulders. With Steve's diamonds around her neck, she was a beautiful picture in a dark frame, as her guests noticed, the men with admiration, the women with envy. She had on her right hand a Mr Thomas Adams, managing director of the new Midland venture, a man of about forty with grey hair and a hard impassive face. He had little conversation and his interest was mainly concentrated on his food. On her other side was a much younger man, a rowing enthusiast, who insisted she must join a rowing club.

'But I don't row,' Noelle objected.

'That doesn't matter, the social side is quite amusing—dances and all that. Were you at Henley?'

Since regatta week had been before her marriage, she told him she had not been in the vicinity, and he insisted she must make a point of going next year . . . next year, would she still be at Forest Lodge, she wondered, living in semi-isolation? Perhaps she had better join a club of some sort, but she was not enthusiastic. Pickles had been banished from the scene, his manners being too exuberant to permit of a public appearance.

Lady Falconbridge from the other end of the table was holding forth to the woman opposite to her, her high voice rising above the general conversation.

'Maternal instinct be damned! I've never suffered from it, I don't believe civilised women do.'

'But you've got lovely twin boys,' someone said.

'Yes, wasn't I lucky? Heir apparent and heir presumptive both at one go, now I need never miss another hunting season.'

Noelle caught the flash of contempt on Ilse's face as the maid offered her a dish of sauté potatoes, to be instantly replaced by the impassivity demanded of a waitress. The German girl was a better woman than the titled lady. She heard Steve's satirical comment:

'And of course with a good nannie and prep schools lined up you won't have to bother further with them.'

'No, thank God.'

Didn't she love her children, Noelle thought, and was Steve equally coldhearted? How she would love to have twin boys, but there did not seem to be any chance of that the way she was living.

The dessert having been served and eaten, she remembered it was up to her to give the signal to leave the table. With a smile at her nearest neighbours, she rose to her feet.

'Coffee will be served in the drawing-room, shall we go?'

Though the convention of leaving the men to their port was no longer observed, Steve called to several of his special cronies to remain with him at the table, as Noelle led the way into the other room. Some of the guests wanted to play cards, others seemed content to sit and smoke in replete somnolence, and listen to the stereogram. Noelle found the room close and oppressive, for the weather had turned unreasonably mild. She wondered if she would be missed if she slipped upstairs to get an aspirin, because her head was aching. Deciding to chance it, she unobtrusively left the room, and nobody seemed to notice her departure. She ran upstairs and was assailed by a sudden giddiness so that she had to clutch at her bedroom door handle for support.

Mrs Ingram was making a final check that the guest-rooms had towels and soap and saw her leaning against the door and hurried to her side.

'You aren't well, madam?'

'Just a little dizzy, it's so hot in the drawing-room.'

The housekeeper opened the bedroom door and gently pushed her inside.

'Sit you down. You've let this party get on top of you. You worry too much, madam.'

Pickles was on the bed, he always took refuge there when Noelle was absent. He growled at the housekeeper, then leaped down and fawned at Noelle's feet as she sank into a chair.

'That dratted dog,' Mrs Ingrams exclaimed, 'messing up your eiderdown!'

'It can be cleaned.' Noelle caressed the dog's head. 'No, Pickles, mind my dress. Could you get me an aspirin, Mrs Ingram, they're in the drawer of the bedside table, and a glass of water.'

Mrs Ingram complied. 'You wouldn't like something stronger? A drop of brandy? I can soon fetch it.'

'No, thank you. I'll be all right in a minute, and I must go back. My husband won't be pleased if I'm not there to see the guests off.'

'They'll not be going just yet.' She looked with concern at Noelle's pale face. 'You don't think you could be expecting, madam?'

Noelle stared at her. 'You mean . . . pregnant?'

'Could be. Often makes you feel poorly to begin with.'

'Oh no, I'm sure . . .' She broke off. It could be. She had tried to forget that devastating night, since it was not something she wished to dwell upon, but nature, that unconscious humorist, had achieved her purpose and it might have borne fruit.

'Might I suggest you see your doctor?' said Mrs Ingram.

'But . . . but it's much too soon . . .'

'They can take tests, you know.'

'Oh yes . . . I'll make an appointment.'

How would Steve react? She still did not know if he wanted a family. She recalled the conversation at the dinner table, nannies and prep schools, but she would tend her child herself, whatever Steve said. She drew a long breath. If he had given her a baby it would make up for everything.

'You'll need to look after yourself, madam,' Mrs Ingram warned her. 'You don't look all that strong.' Then her natural feelings overcame her. 'Eh, but it'll be grand to have a little one in the house, and the master, he'll be that pleased.'

Noelle was not sure about that. 'Please don't tell him,' she said quickly, then seeing the woman's shocked face, 'I . . . I mean, until it's confirmed. He might be disappointed if it's a false alarm.'

'Yes, perhaps you're right,' Mrs Ingram agreed reluctantly. A puzzled crease appeared between her brows. She had expected that Noelle would be eager to share her hope with her husband, and that he would accompany her to the doctor, instead of which she looked as though she didn't want to confide in him. But their relationship was not all it should be, for Steve continued to occupy a separate bedroom. He said his comings and goings were so erratic, he preferred not to disturb his wife with his odd hours—a flimsy excuse. She looked at Noelle darkly; was it possible the child was not his and that was why they were estranged? Or had he had to marry her because she had conceived?

Naturally quite unaware of her housekeeper's unwarranted suspicions, Noelle stood up.

'I must go back. Ask Ilse to put Pickles out for his last run.' Ilse was the only member of the staff the dog tolerated.

'Yes, madam, but hadn't you better go to bed? I'll make your excuses.'

'Oh, no, no!' She could not fail Steve on this her first public appearance, so to speak, though she looked longingly at the wide bed. She had to escort the ladies who were staying to their rooms and make sure they had all they wanted, and bid those who were departing farewell.

As she descended the stairs, she saw Steve standing at the foot of them, waiting for her. She had an urge to run to him and blurt out her suspicion, but he was watching her with a forbidding frown, and the impulse died.

'Where have you been?' he demanded. 'The Falconbridges are leaving and want to say goodbye.'

'I'm sorry,' she said mechanically. 'I went to get an aspirin.'

He looked at her keenly. 'Anything wrong?'

She was level with him now. The top of her head just reached his chin. How handsome he was—those fine aquiline features, the proud way he carried himself, but how remote. She found she could not raise her head to meet his eyes.

'Oh no, just the beginning of a headache.'

'You're pale as a ghost.'

'It's the dress. You wanted me to wear white, it . . . it seems to absorb my colours.'

She did not realise what an utter contrast she was presenting to the laughing, vivid girl he had surprised with Simon by the river. Not only was she pale, but there were shadows beneath her eyes. She saw the frown return and thought he was impatient with her for her delay; she hastened into the drawing room to speed the departing guests. She felt that by conceiving she had committed an indiscretion, and it would be an impertinence to tell this aloof stranger he was going to become a father, but Mrs Ingram's supposition might be incorrect, and there was no point in getting worked up until she had verification.

Most of those guests who had stayed overnight had

breakfast in their rooms, but Noelle thought she had better put in an appearance in the dining room. Steve was there, Mr and Mrs Adams and another couple. Her husband greeted her perfunctorily, and gave her a penetrating look. She did not want any food, as she was feeling queasy—another sign, she thought as she played with a piece of toast. She hoped that when the last visitors had gone, he would give her a word of praise for the night's entertainment, for she had done her best to please him, or would he take it all for granted?

'You're not eating anything,' he said brusquely.

She thought he looked tired and he seemed irritable. Could he suspect?

'I never eat much breakfast,' she reminded him.

Mrs Adams looked at her enviously.

'You don't have to worry about your figure.'

'She's too thin,' Steve commented, as if she deliberately starved herself to annoy him. The look he gave her was almost inimical.

Emma Adams told her: 'I expect Steve has told you we're flying over to Holland tomorrow. Why don't you come too?'

Noelle glanced reproachfully at her husband. It was the first she had heard of it.

'It was a sudden decision,' Steve explained. 'We're angling for a Dutch contract. I'm going back with Adams tonight, as we have to make an early start.'

'I can easily put you both up,' Emma offered. 'And you'd like den Haag. The men will be busy, of course, but I'll show you round.'

Before Noelle could reply, Steve cut in.

'That's very good of you, Emma, but Noelle hasn't

got over her Egyptian trip yet. Perhaps another time.'

Obviously he did not want her to go with him, perhaps he feared complications over sleeping arrangements. Could passion revolt from what it had once desired? It was a painful thought that that might have happened with him.

'How long will you be gone?' Noelle asked, thinking of what she might have to tell him.

'Until Wednesday night.' He handed her a card. 'That's where I'll be staying if any emergency arises.'

She looked a little blankly at the piece of paste-board. She would have liked very much to have gone, but she could hardly say so in the face of his refusal.

'You've packed?'

He had. He always did it himself, scorning to employ a valet. Mrs Ingram looked after his ward-robe; when she had suggested it should be Noelle's chore, he had said the arrangement had worked very efficiently and saw no reason to change it, so she, the wife, was barred from such intimate service, and she was too shy to assert herself.

Noelle waited to say goodbye in the hall while they went to collect their overnight cases. Steve was the first one to return.

As he came downstairs she noticed he was looking drawn, even haggard, there were lines on his face there had never been before, and she cried impulsively:

'You're wearing yourself out. Must you go, can't Mr Adams manage without you so you can have a rest?'

'Good God, I can't find any rest here,' he exclaimed savagely. 'Work is my salvation.'

This outburst bewildered and wounded her. What was wrong with Forest Lodge that he could not relax there? It was quiet and peaceful. She could only surmise that his restless nature could not endure peace and quiet, yet he looked in need of both.

'Oh, Steve . . .' she began, but he interrupted her.

'Sorry about that, but I'm a bit on edge.' He passed his hand wearily across his brow. 'I have to make a very important decision, and it's causing me some sleepless nights.'

'If only I could help!'

'You least of all, my love.'

The Adams couple came creaking down the stairs. They were a weighty pair.

'A pity you can't come,' said Emma as they shook hands. She had noticed Noelle's wistful expression. 'I always go with Tom if it's humanly possible. He needs my moral support.'

But Steve didn't need her in any capacity, Noelle thought sadly.

For appearances' sake, Steve brushed her cheek with his lips, which she noticed were hot and dry. Was he going to be ill? She had never known him be so, and he would be a terribly trying patient, but it might bring them nearer together.

Then they were gone and she was once more alone with Pickles. She went to ring up the doctor.

He saw her that same day. He was a fatherly person who had attended the Prescott household for many years, though Steve only saw him when he required an injection. He thought Noelle probably was pregnant, and he would let her know as soon as possible if the tests were positive.

It was not until Steve had gone that Noelle remembered that she had not mentioned Mrs Bates's revelations and that Steve's cheque was still in her handbag. Mrs Ingram's suggestion had driven the matter clean out of her head. A little delay did not matter, but he might be wondering why the cheque had never been presented. She could in the meantime write to Mary, which she did, saying how glad she was that her illness had been nothing serious. That brought the days on the *Serapis* vividly back to mind. On the whole Steve had been thoughtful and kind, except for the intrusion of Marcia. If only she had not been there, Noelle thought, and they had been able to complete the expedition up the Nile, they might by the end of it have arrived at a closer understanding. For Steve had wanted her then, and only her timidity had stood between them. That and her pride, which Marcia's presence had aggravated. Poor Steve, he had had rather a raw deal, expecting a voluptuous lover and being confronted with a shrinking virgin. She smiled wryly, recalling their wedding night. But when he had consummated their marriage it had been in anger and as a punishment, and that brought her back to the present, for how was he going to react when faced with the consequences of his unleashed passion?

On the Wednesday night, he returned as he said he would and was in time for dinner. He looked much less tired, but was cool and detached. No, he had not seen much of Holland, he told Noelle in answer to her polite queries, he was in conference most of the time, and den Haag, though a pleasant place in the summer, was bleak at that time of the year. When she diffidently asked if he had reached a decision about the problem that had been worrying him, he smiled a trifle sourly and said that he had.

'I'll tell you about that over coffee,' he promised her.

Noelle felt a thrill of elation. Was he at last going to take her into his confidence?

She had put on one of her most becoming dresses, a saxe blue creation that brought out the colour of her eyes. It fitted closely over waist and hips, and she reflected that if she were pregnant, she would not be able to wear it very much longer. Would Steve be put out that his decorative piece was going to be spoilt?

She had put Mrs Bates' letter and the cheque in the little silver brocade bag she used in the evenings, and she told him:

'I also have something to tell you.'

She must return the cheque to him and make her apologies.

'Quite a conference, my love,' Steve suggested with his crooked smile. 'Perhaps we'll need something stronger than coffee.'

'Have a cognac if you like, but coffee will do for me.'

They went into the drawing room, and Noelle seated herself behind the coffee tray. As usual she made a charming picture, as she handed him his cup, her full skirt spread over the velvet covering of the sofa, and Pickles lying at her feet. Steve, in a chair opposite to her, looked at her with a curious expression, then sighed and put down his cup.

'I'm afraid I made a big mistake when I persuaded you to marry me,' he said abruptly.

His remark was so totally unexpected that Noelle could only stare at him blankly. Pickles sat up and scratched an ear.

Steve sighed again, drained his cup, and put it down beside him. Then he went on:

'It's perfectly obvious to me that you're not happy. I . . . I'm not the right man for you, I'm too mature. You should marry someone more like the boy you lost. Does he still haunt you?'

'No. Oh, no.' She had not thought of Hugh for some time now, but she had spoken his name on her wedding night, and that was what Steve was remembering.

'You could meet another like him,' Steve said a little contemptuously—he had never had much opinion of Hugh, 'but as for myself, I've not been as . . . er . . . considerate as I might, I must admit, but I thought you were far more sophisticated than you are and much more . . . er . . . experienced. I'm afraid I've shocked and scared you more than once.'

Noelle moistened her lips with the tip of her tongue.

'What you mean is, you find me inadequate.'

'Not at all. You behaved beautifully at our house party and looked lovely, but you didn't really enjoy it, did you?'

'It was a bit of an ordeal,' she admitted unwillingly. 'They were all strangers.'

'And not your contemporaries. Not at all the sort of company you're used to, my love.'

But not as out of place as Steve would have appeared at one of the disco sessions she, Hugh and Simon had gone to when feeling a need for recreation. How juvenile they seemed now!'

'I'll get used . . .' she began.

'I don't want any more sacrifices from you,' he interrupted her. Pickles came and sat up on his hind legs by the coffee table. Absently she began to feed him with sugar as Steve went on:

'When I saw you with Simon that Sunday, you were a different person. I realised then the wrong I'd done you. Oh, you've been honest, you never pretended to love me,' he dropped his voice. 'That might have made a difference.

'But you . . . you don't want love.'

'I believe it's important to a woman when it comes to sex,' he said bluntly. 'Oh, stop giving that dog sugar, he'll be sick.' The irritability in his tone betrayed that he was not as calm as he was trying to appear.

'I wasn't thinking . . . No, Pickles, no more.' Should she confess that she had come to love him? But he had not finished. She had better hear him out before she did anything desperate.

Steve continued in a hard, matter-of-fact voice:

'The long and the short of it is that I've decided to give you your freedom. I will, of course, provide for you adequately, if you want to start a boutique, I'll finance it, but as for living together—well, it's become rather a farce, hasn't it?'

That was his fault, he was never at home. Her mind instantly flew to the obvious explanation.

'You mean you've found someone else, who'll suit you better?'

'Naturally you would think that. You've always believed I'm some sort of sex maniac,' he said bitterly.

'You need women, and in that respect I know I've been a complete failure,' she acknowledged sadly.

'As I said, we're not suited, and I'm sure you'll be glad to be rid of a callous brute.'

'Oh no, Steve, you're not that. I ... I've called you some hard things, and they weren't justified, that I've just found out.' She fumbled in her bag and held out the cheque. 'It was partly your own fault, you always let me think the worst. Why didn't you tell me about that?'

He took it, looked at it and laughed.

'So he's returned it.'

'He didn't need it, but it was a kind thought. Why do you persist in pretending you don't care about other people's difficulties?'

Steve tore the cheque into small pieces before he replied.

'They were your friends, so I did what I could to compensate for refusing to allow you to see them again. That was a risk I wouldn't permit you to take, but had I told you what I'd done, you might feel you had to prostitute yourself out of gratitude.' Noelle made a small sound of dissent, but he held up his hand. 'Let me continue. Throughout our association you've tried to do what you considered to be your duty, even submitting to my ...' his mouth twisted satirically '... base lusts. You couldn't help it if your body rebelled, but I keep telling you I don't care for sacrifices. I had hoped that if we were married ... but never mind that now. It hasn't worked out, so we'd better cut our losses.'

He spoke without any sign of emotion, so that Noelle could not bring herself to utter the frantic protests that rose to her lips. Steve had called her an icicle, but he was an iceberg, sitting there announcing his decision as if he were presiding at a board meeting. How could you tell a man that you had come to love him, when he had told you that he wanted to be rid of you? For that was what he was saying. She had failed him and he had no use for failures. She was too young, too naïve for the position he wanted her to fill, and the sight of her in jeans and torn sweater had offended his fastidiousness. Steven Prescott's wife should always appear well gowned and poised. But that was only a minor matter. What he could not forgive was that she had failed to respond to his lovemaking, had not fallen in love with him during those courtship days now so far away, and on her wedding night had spoken another man's name.

'Steve, I . . . I've changed . . . can't we . . .'

He cut her short. 'Don't feel you have to make insincere protestations to appease my . . . er . . . masculine vanity, because you feel indebted to me.' He smiled wryly. 'You've told me far too often in unguarded moments that you consider I'm an uncivilised brute, and perhaps I am. I came from the people, and I'm a red-blooded man without the refinements of someone like your Hugh, who, forgive me saying so, seemed to me to be a bit of a wet. How he could associate with you intimately for years and not bed you passes my understanding. Fortunately the world is full of other women less delicately minded, who find pleasure in satisfying . . . my lusts. So you need not reproach yourself, my love, for having deprived me.'

Stung, Noelle said, her voice shaking:

'Hadn't you better stop calling me your love, since I never have and never will be that?'

'As you please.' He was superbly indifferent. 'I shall be off again tomorrow, but I'll be back on Saturday. Perhaps you'll think over all I've said, and tell me then what you'd like to do.' He stood up. 'Incidentally, I will of course continue to pay for Simon's training. I like the lad and he deserves a good start. Your father's position is quite secure, you need have no uneasiness about them. Goodnight.'

So he had been well aware of her reasons for marrying him. He must think she was a mercenary . . . cheat! She sprang to her feet, hot tears coursing down her cheeks.

'Steve . . .'

Perhaps she deserved all he had said, but all that was past, and she could not contemplate a future without him.

'Steve . . . please!'

He looked with distaste at her ruined make-up.

'Oh, don't make a scene,' he said wearily. 'There's nothing to cry about; I've told you you'll be well provided for, and you'll be rid of me.'

Pride raised its battered head.

'I won't take a penny of your money,' she declared fiercely. 'I earned my own living before I married you and I can again.'

'Don't be absurd!'

'It's not absurd. If you support me I . . . I'll be a kept woman. I won't descend to that.'

Steve grinned at her description.

'Not that, my . . . Noelle. I'll make no demands on you, but you can't model for ever, I'm providing for your old age.'

'I hope I'll be dead before then,' she cried stormily.

'What drama, when you've a carefree and untrammelled existence opening before you.' He was mocking her, and Noelle made an effort to recover her poise. 'Think it over,' he went on, 'and we'll talk again when I return on Saturday, by which time I'm sure you'll have become reconciled to your lot.'

He was gone. Noelle collapsed on the sofa, weeping copiously. Pickles climbed up on to her lap and tried to lick away her tears, and she hugged his warm wriggling body. In her perturbation during the scene with Steve, she had forgotten all about her visit to the doctor and what he might have to tell her. She remembered it now; that was a complication Steve had not foreseen. If he did not want the child, she did, and she would certainly have to accept his support, however much it riled her pride.

On Friday morning the doctor rang up, to confirm her pregnancy.

CHAPTER ELEVEN

NOELLE awaited Steve's arrival on that fateful Saturday with considerable trepidation. The future was no longer her decision but his. If he wanted the child he would not let her go, at any rate until it was born, and she would not leave him then if it meant she must give it up. But he might not, because for all she knew he might have formed another connection with someone more suited to him, who he intended should supersede her, when the divorce had been made absolute. That seemed more than likely, and he would not want to wait the couple of years before he or she could claim desertion. That meant that she would have to proceed against him for infidelity, which she did not believe she could ever bring herself to do, though she might for the baby's sake, because then it would be wholly hers, to bring up as she chose, without the shadows of nannies and boarding schools hanging over it. The idea was not without its attraction, for though she would lose Steve, who did not want her, she would retain a part of him in his child, but as it was his child, he had a right to know of its inception, and that was what she must tell him when she saw him again.

She still felt painfully shy about doing so, especially as she did not know how he would react. They had drawn so far apart—not that they had ever been close, it seemed almost indecent to inform him of her condition. The awful thought occurred to her that he might possibly doubt that it was his—though she did not see how he could entertain such an idea, for he had discovered she was a virgin when he had taken her, and there had been no one else.

Unfortunately he had such a low opinion of women, he might suspect that she had avenged herself for his neglect by playing Lady Chatterley with someone on the estate during his frequent absences, but if he were cad enough to do that, she would most certainly leave him, however much it hurt her, and bring up her child far from his pernicious influence.

Again she might be wronging him. He had told

her more than once not to be too hasty in her judgments, appearances could be deceptive, and Mrs Bates' letter had been one instance of proving her conclusions to be entirely incorrect, but how could a girl be fair to a man who consistently refused to explain himself? If she loved she should trust, but that was the hell of it, she couldn't give him blind trust, when he did nothing to earn it. He had said that if he told her what he had done for the Bates, he feared she would have felt under an obligation to him which she must discharge in ways distasteful to her, an involved and not very convincing excuse. He had said upon another occasion that he did not want gratitude, then what *did* he want? For he had also jeered at falling in love, so it would not please him to learn that she had and was, and he would no doubt attribute some devious motive to her declaration of a change of heart. There seemed to be no way at all in which she could break through to him. Only someone like Marcia could do that, she thought bitterly. They understood each other, being two of a kind, but whatever she did or said Steve took the wrong way.

Marcia had been back in England for some time, and he expected to run across her, if he had not already done so. He might be with her now, for he was so secretive about where he was going and who with. Business involvement could cover a multitude of diversions, from the proverbial 'being kept late at the office', to cover amorous liaisons or illicit trips abroad, while the deceived wife remained in ignorance at home.

Yet whatever he did and was, her love for him

continued to grow. He had got under her skin, invaded her imagination. For all his faults, Steve was indisputably a ruler of men, a born leader, having fought his way up to the top of the tree. Noelle was reminded of a statue of the great Rameses, with Nefertari, the beloved wife, beside him, but only coming up to his knee. That was how she felt with Steve.

But none of these unhappy reflections solved the problem of how to disclose her news to her husband. It seemed so bald to say: 'I'm going to have a baby.' And the night it had been conceived was something they both pretended hadn't happened, Steve because he was a little ashamed of his violence, and she because the memory smirched her fastidious sensitiveness. She had not been entirely unresponsive, but it had not been love between them.

Then she hit upon a bright idea that would tell him without any spoken word at all. She had herself driven into Maidenhead, for though she could drive—Hugh had taught her—she was never very confident on the traffic-laden roads, and Steve much preferred that she utilised the chauffeur.

I must get myself a little car and with practice I'll become more expert, she mused, as the limousine rolled smoothly towards its destination. I'll need some sort of transport, if . . . a big if.

Noelle purchased wool, needles and pattern books. She was not a good knitter, but that again was something she must practise. She could buy layettes by the dozen if she so wished, but with Steve's money, and she liked to feel she was doing something personal to welcome the newcomer.

When Steve came in on the Saturday afternoon, he found his wife seated upon the sofa, concentrating upon a half-finished infant's vest, with sheaves of pattern books strewn around her. Pickles rushed to give him an enthusiastic welcome, and after he had quieted the dog she looked up with a slightly self-conscious smile:

'Hi, Steve, everything going well?' And promptly dropped a stitch.

'Yes, thanks.' He seemed fascinated by her busy fingers. 'I didn't know you were keen on knitting.'

'It passes the time.'

In case he hadn't got the message, she ostentatiously picked up a pattern book with a picture of a grinning baby on the cover.

'Is that for . . . a friend?'

Noelle counted stitches, then said deliberately:

'No one I know is having a baby.'

He stared at her incredulously, and she blushed vividly, giving the game away.

'Noelle!'

He came towards her, snatching the knitting from her hands and casting it aside, where it was promptly retrieved by Pickles, who carried it off in triumph to his basket. Steve had seized both of Noelle's wrists.

'Look at me!'

Slowly Noelle raised her eyes to meet the penetrating grey ones, while the colour deepened to cover both face and neck.

'Yes,' she said simply.

'But . . . how?'

She could see he was thinking back, back to that night on the *Serapis*, and a little prick of resentment pierced her. Did men never think of consequences until they were thrust upon them? She said calmly:

'This is the punishment you inflicted upon me.'

'Oh, my love, don't say that!' Steve dropped on his knees beside her, his arms encircling her waist, and buried his face in her lap. Noelle stared down at the dark head upon her skirt, completely overcome. This display of feeling from one who never showed feeling except in moments of passion was entirely unexpected. Tentatively she stroked his hair, still so thick and dark; age cannot wither him . . . no, that was said of a woman, Cleopatra. The emotion surging through him communicated itself to her in the close holding of his arms. And she had believed he was cold! Half laughing, half crying, because she was deeply moved, she complained:

'You . . . and Pickles . . . have ruined my knitting.'

'Damn your knitting,' his voice was muffled. 'What a thing to be thinking of at a time like this!'

He looked up at her and his eyes were soft as morning mist, because they were wet.

'God is good. I didn't dare hope for this.'

More and more astonished, for she hadn't thought Steve believed in God, she murmured:

'I gather you're . . . pleased?'

'Aren't you? Or are you another Lady Falconbridge who considers procreation an unpleasant necessity?'

'Don't mention that unnatural female! It's what I've always wanted.'

His arms tightened about her waist.

'Even though I'll never, never let you go now. You're caught . . . trapped.' There was triumph in his voice. This was the old Steve, the one she knew.

'But I don't want to go. I thought *you* wanted to be rid of *me*.'

'Good God, whatever gave you that idea?'

'You haven't been exactly matey since we came back here.'

Keep it light, instinct warned her, aware they were hovering on the edge of an abyss. His passion for her was not dead after all, she could feel it in the close grip of his arms, see it in the smouldering fire which had come into his grey eyes. Deep within her, a flame leaped in response, but that wasn't the answer. They had to come to an understanding first.

Pickles, puzzled by their unusual behaviour, abandoned Noelle's knitting which he had been happily chewing, and came to push an enquiring nose between them. His action broke the mounting tension.

'Damned dog!' Steve exclaimed, and rose to his feet. He stood looking down at her. 'When did you know?'

'The night of the party. I felt poorly and Mrs Ingram told me to see a doctor. He confirmed it yesterday morning.'

'You might have told me.'

'Well, I wasn't sure and you'd other things on your mind. You were going to Holland.'

'You've got your priorities wrong, but yesterday morning, you could have phoned the office.'

'I didn't know if you'd be there . . . or if you'd be pleased.'

He thrust his hands into his trouser pockets and began to pace the room. His face had regained its normal closed expression, he was completely in control of himself again.

'You realise what this means, Noelle? As I said, I

won't let you go now. You may hate and despise me, but as the mother of my child, you should be here with me.'

'Steve!' Noelle sprang to her feet. She went and stood in front of him to stop his restless pacing. 'I neither hate you nor despise you. You're obstinate, difficult and totally blind, but I love you, faults and all.'

He stopped and stared at her. 'What did you say?'

'I love you,' she repeated it steadily. 'I know you don't think much of love, but you'll have to accept it.' She smiled wistfully, her big eyes full of tenderness. 'You said once no one had loved you for yourself alone, but I do. I don't care a ha'penny about big houses, mink coats and diamonds, I'd be happy with you in a cottage. Happier, because then I could look after you, cook and wash and mend your socks. Much happier, because then I'd feel I was necessary to you.'

'But you are, only I was sure I revolted you, you thought I was a coarse brute. You said you didn't love me when I married you.'

'I didn't then . . .'

'And you could never forget Hugh Forbes.'

'No more I shall,' she said quietly. 'But that part of my life is over. I've grown so much since then, and what I feel for you is different, much stronger.'

He was unconvinced. 'You changed very suddenly.'

'I think it was Marcia who did it,' she said meditatively. 'Her pursuit of you showed me my true feelings, but you seemed to care more for her than me, and . . .' a glint of mischief came into her eyes, 'I didn't appreciate having to share my husband.'

'From the way you behaved on our wedding night, I didn't think you wanted a husband at all.'

'I was afraid of you,' she admitted frankly, 'and as

you afterwards discovered, I'd never slept with a man before. But that's past history.' Summoning all her courage, she looked straight into his eyes, very pale and serious. 'If we're going to go on living together, I can't stand any more of this semi-detached existence.'

'Good God, do you think it was by my wish? I hardly dared to sleep in the house, knowing you were there and I wanted you so. But I'd sworn to myself I'd never molest you again without an invitation after that night on the *Serapis* when my temper go the better of me.'

So that was why he had been so distant, so aloof—and she had thought he had lost interest in her.

Her mouth curved in an enchanting smile, as she told him:

'Well, I'm glad it did, since there's to be such a happy sequel.'

'Oh, my love!' Quite a different inflection this time. His arms enclosed her. 'So I'm forgiven?'

'For that, yes, a long time ago.'

'And you meant what you said, no more separate rooms?' Steve looked at her questioningly, still fearful of a rebuff.

'It was very lonely in that big bed,' she sighed, 'but I still can't believe that you really want me.'

'Want you!' he exclaimed, his arms tightening. 'I've felt like Tantalus, always the water was there before me, but I dared not drink. The only relief I could find was to go away, and then I was itching to return . . . to the blue room.'

Noelle's arms were about his neck, and she whispered in his ear:

'We'll move your things, no more blue room for you.'

'Thank God for that!'

He sank down on the sofa, drawing her across his knees. They clung together, and at last their lips met.

Noelle felt tides of rapture surge over her, all the sweeter for having been denied so long.

Presently Steve lifted his head and said unsteadily:

'I'm forgetting the baby. Perhaps I should continue in my old quarters until it's born.'

'And condemn me to eight months solitary?' Noelle protested. 'I need you, Steve, to sustain and support me.'

'Bless you, my darling, for those kind words. I'll do that and more.' Tenderly he smoothed the loosened hair back from her forehead. 'If we have a daughter I hope she has hair like yours.'

'More likely to be dark, like you. If she is, I'll call her Nefertari.'

'You will not! Think how she'd be ragged at school with a label like that. So our Egyptian holiday wasn't an entire loss.'

'Far from it, but Steve, there's something I've wondered about.'

'Yes?'

She felt his muscles tauten apprehensively, but she wanted to set her mind at rest about what had always irked her. It seemed she had been so wrong about many things, and it might be she was mistaken about that too.

'It won't make any difference now, but I'd like a truthful answer, and I may have misjudged you.'

'You probably have. What is this momentous question?'

'Did you go to Marcia on our wedding night when you said you would seek a more welcoming bed?'

Steve laughed. 'Has that been rankling all this while? Of course I didn't, I'd no idea she was in

Egypt. I said that because I was frustrated and disappointed. Actually I walked about all night.' He drew away from her and went on earnestly: 'Noelle, this is the truth. I did have an affair with Marcia a long time ago, but since I met you there's been no other woman. I played up to her on the *Serapis* in the hope of making you jealous, but I never slept with her, though you thought I did, didn't you?' Noelle flushed and turned away her head. 'I don't blame you, it was those deceptive appearances again. I wanted you from our first meeting, but you were involved with Hugh Forbes. When he died, I was determined to marry you myself. You consented eventually, though I knew you agreed more for your family's sake than from inclination. In my arrogance I thought I could soon displace Hugh's memory and win your love. To be frank, no other woman I'd desired had ever resisted me.'

'Bad lad,' Noelle murmured softly, and stroked his face.

'I've never pretended to be a saint, but you continued to hold aloof. It maddened me. When it seemed you preferred ben Ahmed, I could have killed you both. I did nearly kill you.' He sighed ruefully. 'Because of that, when we came back here, I thought I'd alienated you entirely. So I kept out of your way. I nearly broke my resolution once, that night I gave you the necklace—you seemed to be melting, and then that damned woman rang up.'

'Your . . . your secretary?'

'Yes. Poor girl, she was only doing her duty.'

Noelle was glad he did not know what she had surmised about that. She asked anxiously:

'But what made you decide we should part?'

'Simon. I could see you weren't happy. Then

when I saw you with your brother, I realised what I was doing to you, I was destroying your youth, but it was not too late for it to revive in a different environment, away from me. The only amends I could make was to set you free. I'd come to care much more for your happiness than for myself.'

'That,' said Noelle with shining eyes, 'is true love.'

'Is it? You must teach me about this love business, Noelle, you know more about it than I do.'

'You don't need any tuition.' For he had passed the test, that of putting the beloved's welfare before his own.

Pickles, one ear up, one ear down, brought the mangled knitting to lay at their feet to attract their attention.

Steve picked it up and laughed.

'Hardly worthy of our offspring, is it?'

'I . . . I didn't know how to tell you.'

He looked at her reproachfully.

'My love, are you still afraid of me?'

She shook her head. 'Never any more.'

Steve rose to his feet, holding out his hand. 'Come, let's go and look at those nurseries. They'll have to be redecorated. As for you, you rascal,' he looked down at Pickles, 'you're not on in this act—go basket!'

Pickles knew who was master in that house and turned to obey, tail between legs, but Noelle cried:

'Oh, let him come too, he's one of the family and I want him to be friends with the baby.'

Steve made no further demur, and hand in hand they went out of the room and up the broad staircase, with the little dog pattering at their heels.